Broken Lives and Other Stories

This series of publications on Africa, Latin America, Southeast Asia, and Global and Comparative Studies is designed to present significant research, translation, and opinion to area specialists and to a wide community of persons interested in world affairs. The editor seeks manuscripts of quality on any subject and can usually make a decision regarding publication within three months of receipt of the original work. Production methods generally permit a work to appear within one year of acceptance. The editor works closely with authors to produce a high-quality book. The series appears in a paperback format and is distributed worldwide. For more information, contact the executive editor at Ohio University Press, Scott Quadrangle, University Terrace, Athens, Ohio 45701.

Executive editor: Gillian Berchowitz
AREA CONSULTANTS
Africa: Diane M. Ciekawy
Latin America: Thomas Walker
Southeast Asia: William H. Frederick
Global and Comparative Studies: Ann R. Tickamyer

Broken Lives and Other Stories

Anthonia C. Kalu

Foreword by Emmanuel N. Obiechina

Ohio University Research in International Studies
Africa Series No. 79
Ohio University Press
Athens

© 2003 by the Center for International Studies
Ohio University
Printed in the United States of America
All rights reserved

12 11 10 09 08 07 06 05 04 03   5 4 3 2 1

The books in the Ohio University Research in International Studies Series
are printed on acid-free paper ∞

Published in the United States of America by Ohio University Press,
Athens, Ohio 45701

Library of Congress Cataloging-in-Publication Data

Kalu, Anthonia C.
  Broken lives and other stories / Anthonia C. Kalu ; with an introduction by
Emmanuel N. Obiechina.
    p.   cm. – (Ohio University research in international studies. Africa series ;
no. 79)
    Contents: Independence – Angelus – The last push – Camwood – Broken lives
– Children's day – Ogbanje father – Relief duty – Osondu – The gift.
    ISBN 0-89680-229-9
    1. Nigeria—History—Civil War, 1967-1970—Fiction.   2. War victims—Fic-
tion.   I. Title.   II. Research in international studies. Africa series ; no. 79.

PS3611.A755B76 2003
813'6—dc21   2003043362

For:

My parents, Margaret M. and Peter K. Ogbonaya

My husband, Kelechi

and

All the Sons and Daughters of Ututu

Contents

Foreword by Emmanuel N. Obiechina, *ix*

Preface, *xxi*

Independence, *1*

Angelus, *20*

The Last Push, *44*

Camwood, *64*

Broken Lives, *88*

Children's Day, *106*

Ogbanje Father, *124*

Relief Duty, *146*

Osondu, *161*

The Gift, *174*

Glossary, *181*

Foreword

The Nigerian Civil War

Until the Rwandan genocide of 1994, no event of Africa's postcolonial history has attracted as much local and world attention as the Nigerian civil war of July 1967 to January 1970. Also called the Nigeria-Biafra War or simply the Biafran War, it arose from a series of unresolved crises that followed the formal accession of the former British colony of Nigeria to the status of independence on October 1, 1960. There were ethnic and religious conflicts in Nigeria even while the British were still in control, but independence brought conflicts to the boil and added new, more intransigent problems. These conflicts and sociopolitical problems became so serious that security of life and property could no longer be guaranteed by the national government, especially to the people of the former Eastern Region of the country's four federated units. That sector felt itself more adversely affected by the collapse of civic governance and decided to assume responsibility for its own affairs by declaring itself a separate state on May 30, 1967. It named itself the Republic of Biafra, after the Bight of Biafra on its Atlantic coast. Nigeria declared war to force the breakaway region back into the country and thus began the civil war described by historian A. H. M. Kirk-Greene as "the bloodiest civil war of the twentieth century." Biafra was completely blockaded by the Federal side. It was given three weeks to buckle under Federal might but succeeded in defending its independence for thirty months. On January 12, 1970, it gave up the struggle and returned to Nigeria. By then an estimated one to three million people had died, most of them from famine. In the words of Zach Dundas, Biafra was "killed with fire and disease." Material losses were incalculable.

Occurring in an age of communication revolution, the Biafran War itself was well covered by the world's major media; television footage brought images of starving children and bomb-shattered noncombatants into the living rooms of prime-time television viewers in distant parts of the world. It was a war in which outstanding journalists from major world newspapers were involved, a virtual who's who of the international press: Renata Adler of the *New Yorker,* Winston S. Churchill in the *Times of London,* Lloyd Garrison of the *New York Times Magazine,* Michael Leapman of the *New Statesman,* Auberon Waugh in the *Spectator,* and John de St. Jorre of the *Observer,* not to mention Frederick Forsyth, who remained in Biafra after his official BBC assignment was decommissioned by his pro-Federal employers. These journalists had provided eyewitness accounts of the war to their overseas readers, and some had followed up with book-length publications about the war.

Historians and social scientists were not left behind in the effort to document the war, its genesis, and its aftermath. The most outstanding contribution in that regard is Kirk-Greene's two-volume *Crisis and Conflict in Nigeria: A Documentary Sourcebook, 1966–1970* (Oxford 1971), a major compendium of the background to the crises, attempts and failures to resolve them, and the course of the civil war. These are primary documents, that will prove invaluable to historians of the future. Peter Schwab's *Biafra* (New York, 1971) also presents a documentation of events in their barest outline, including the Federal economic blockade of Biafra, the various events of the war, peace efforts, foreign relations, starvation and relief efforts, and the end of the war. The diplomatic maneuvers during the war are covered in such works as Suzanne Cronjé's *The Diplomatic History of the Biafran War, 1967–1970* (London, 1972), a perspicacious study of the diplomatic intrigues, especially of the British Labor Party government, which supplied arms and diplomatic cover to the federal Nigerian side in the civil war. Then there was Auberon Waugh and Suzanne Cronjé's joint book, *Biafra: Britain's Shame*, an outspoken criticism of Britain's position in the civil war, and Dan Jacob's *The Brutality of Nations* (New York, 1987), which describes "how, in pursuit of political objectives in the Nigerian Civil War, a number of great and small nations, including Britain and the United States, worked to prevent supplies of food and medicine from reaching the starving children of rebel Biafra."

Internally, a considerable number of participants in the civil war, on both sides, have left records of their activities during the struggle, often by way of personal memoirs and, implicitly, as a defense or justification of actions or clarifications of contested issues. Among these are books by military and political leaders, civil administrators, and even those involved in the military coup d'état that brought the army into politics for the first time. Of particular interest among the memoirs is *The Man Died: Prison Notes of Wole Soyinka* (Harmondsworth, 1979), containing the account of his nearly two years of solitary confinement without charge by the Federal authorities.

Biafran War Literature

By far the largest concentration of works on the Nigerian civil war has been by creative writers. The works have appeared in all the major genres of literature and some writers have featured works in more than one genre. So strong has been the pull of this event that the flow of creativity that began with the start of the crises in the 1960s is still going on vigorously. The explanation may lie in the fact that the civil war was to a great extent a writers' war. Nigerian writers were drawn into it from the start. Unequal though the war had been from the beginning, the sense of moral outrage at the victimization of citizens by the state drew the sympathy of writers toward the Biafran cause. Most of the major writers of the day—Chinua Achebe, Christopher Okigbo, Cyprian Ekwensi, Gabriel Okara, Flora Nwapa, Michael Echeruo, John Ekwere, Kalu Uka, John Munonye, and Onuora Nzekwu—were involved on the Biafran side. Okigbo, the best lyrical poet of Nigeria, died while on active duty, as a major in the Biafran army. Wole Soyinka, who attempted to play a mediational role as the crises were unfolding, was quickly seized by the Federal authorities and detained. His fate became a warning to all would-be peacebrokers that the field was irredeemably polarized. The first and subsequent generations of Nigerian writers produced works that explore themes relating to the war, the crises that led to it, its beginnings, and the aftermath.

Soon after the end of the war, a collection of short stories titled *The Insider: Stories of War and Peace from Nigeria* (Enugu, Nigeria, 1971), edited by Chinua Achebe and others, was issued by a newly formed publishing company in Enugu, the former Biafran capital. The stories revealed the angst and scars of the war so clearly evident in its survivors. Fiction accounts for the largest body of the war literature. The urge to tell this painful story has remained strong in those who went through the excruciating experiences, as it was in those who had felt the effects of the war vicariously. Among the fictional works are Chinua Achebe's *Girls at War and Other Stories* (London, 1977), S. O. Mezu's *Behind the Rising Sun* (London, 1971), I. N. C. Aniebo's *The Anonymity of Sacrifice* (London, 1974), Flora Nwapa's *Never Again* (Enugu, 1975) and *Wives at War and Other Stories* (Enugu, 1980), John Munonye's *A Wreath for the*

Maidens (London, 1976), Cyprian Ekwensi's *Survive the Peace* (London, 1976) and *Divided We Stand* (London, 1976), Chukwuemeka Ike's *Sunset at Dawn* (London, 1976), Isidore Okpewho's *The Last Duty* (Harlow, 1976), Wole Soyinka's *Season of Anomy* (Walton-on-Thames, 1980), Buchi Emecheta's *Destination Biafra* (London, 1982), Elechi Amadi's *Estrangement* (London, 1986), Phanuel Egejuru's *The Seed Yams Have Been Eaten* (Ibadan, 1993), Ken Saro-Wiwa's *Sozaboy: A Novel in Rotten English* (Harlow, 1994), and Ossie Enekwe's *The Last Battle and Other Stories* (Lagos, 1994). Major poetry works are Christopher Okigbo's posthumous *Labyrinths and the Path of Thunder* (London, 1971), Chinua Achebe's *Christmas in Biafra and Other Poems* (New York, 1972), J. P. Clark-Bekederemo's "Casualties" in his *Collected Plays and Poetry* (Washington, D.C., 1991), and Wole Soyinka's *Idanre and Other Poems* (London, 1967) and *A Shuttle in the Crypt* (London, 1972). One major play that emerged from the war experience is Soyinka's absurdist *Madmen and Specialists* in *Six Plays* (London, 1984).

These and many more texts provide a huge creative documentation of the Nigerian civil war as well as varied insights into that monumental tragedy. The question that may well arise is: In view of this huge documentation and exploration of the war, is there anything that another collection of short stories could add to our perception of that civil war? Is another accumulation of images of destruction and atrocities going to enhance our perception of the tragedy? In other words, is another collection of short stories really necessary? The answer, in my opinion, is that it all depends on the collection itself, on the degree of narrative competence and depth of vision brought by the author to bear on the familiar themes and situations. Having read Anthonia Kalu's *Broken Lives and Other Stories*, I am convinced that this is another work that deserves to be known and read extensively. It reveals many fresh perspectives and insights on the civil war that will both enrich and reward the reader.

Broken Lives and Other Stories

Out of the Biafran tragic history, Anthonia Kalu has rescued a human story, isolated specific events, and explored them imaginatively, extracting from them their built-in significances and forcing them, in all manner of subtle ways, to yield their inner meanings and emotive potentialities. These ten short stories are well told by an author who was a mere high school child when the events of the civil war happened. Helped by an exceptional sense of observation and a retentive memory, she had followed the intricacies of the dislocations of the war with such concentration as to be able to reconstruct and weave them into unforgettable tales with extraordinary clarity of vision and insights.

Broken Lives is a subtly structured exploration of the many-layered crises of which the physical wounds and sufferings of the war are only the exposed surface. Below that surface lie embedded realities that enhance the reader's appreciation of the destruction and inner corrosion caused by the war. The surface wounds and suffering are like nothing when compared to the inner psychological wounds of the victims. In this collection, the events of the war are embedded within richly textured cultural matrices that make the reading of the stories a rewarding intellectual experience. It is as if the reader is being offered many significant values, a sensitively constructed narrative and a bonus of cultural education and deep psychological insights, all at the price of a single reading effort. Furthermore, the collection has a unity within which the narratives are linked in a tapestry of logic and internal coherence. Even though the stories are each different, distinct, and self-contained, the ordering of them and their central events and themes relates them in a recognizable whole. The first two stories provide a backdrop of history that anticipates and ultimately leads to the upheavals in postcolonial Biafra. They are followed by seven stories that focus on different but relevantly connected aspects of the civil war and that maximally explore devastation of personal and social life. The final story is an optimistic coda that neatly ties up everything. It looks beyond the devastation and links the peculiarities of the narrator's life to the circumstances of the war's ending and a reconstructed national future.

The collection opens with "Independence," a story in which the world is poised for change from colonial dependency to political freedom. But this change is fraught with uncertainties and the possibilities of both salvation and damnation. It is problematized further by being seen from the perspective of children. The coming of independence brings great excitement, but in the view of children it is something of a threat too—to the established order of life. In spite of the drills and the parades, the ritual of saluting the flag, the dancing and the masquerade, the event leaves considerable foreboding that things will never be the same. The children talk wistfully about independence as the end of the world, their intuition foreshadowing the harsh times that are soon to roll over them. In "Angelus" life is viewed at first through the prism of adolescent optimism, as solemnities dissolve into rampant giggles. We have here endearing portraits of school life, sweet remembrances of foreign teachers and guardians and a few locals bearing the burden of the civilizing enterprise and ministering to bright-eyed young girls. In this intricately woven story we hear the retreating echoes of the old imperial British majesty and idealistic Christian missionaries that had been engaged in the "battle" for the souls of the children—the empire of this world in a struggle with the kingdom of heaven, each demanding allegiance with its ritualistic pressures. Suddenly, the harsh winds of postimperial stress begin to blow into the manicured world of the all-girls high school and fear arrives to disturb the ordered, peaceful tenor of convent life. A sense of crisis and doom transforms adolescents overnight into adults as the chicanery of manipulative politics destroys a major center of national stability. The stage is set for the unfolding of what poet Christopher Okigbo called "this century's brush fire."

"The Last Push" highlights the use of airpower by the Federal side to put Biafra under pressure by carrying the war to noncombatants in churches, schools, marketplaces, and in their homes. This heightens the sense of insecurity everywhere among the people. Life is reduced to a certain precariousness underlined by fatalism that allows no respite and no escape. Death is just around the corner and can come in all manner of ways, including horrible dismemberment. Worse than physical mutilation are the wounds in the souls of the victims, the ever-present fears that make three- and five-year-olds talk in frightened whispers about the bombings and strafings, the "take-cover," as they popularly called the phenomenon. And worse than the fears and uncertainties is the corrosive effect of the alternation of hope and despair playing against each other in a tantalizing game of approach-and-retreat. Biafra was recognized by four African countries—Tanzania, Ivory Coast, Gabon, and Zambia—and the Caribbean island country of Haiti. Each recognition brought a surge of hope that the war would soon come to an end, and each time the people celebrated the event, which invariably would be followed by greater efforts on the part of the Federal army to defeat Biafra militarily, which in turn meant greater brutality, more deaths, greater depression among the Biafrans attempting to sustain their independence. The author captures this invidious situation in her supple style:

> After Gabon recognized the new Biafra, everybody and their mother danced the recognition dance. It was a war dance of recognition that Chika and her friends danced that day, thinking it meant the end of the war. But like most things brought by the war, it turned out to be the beginning of months of fear, uncertainty, hunger, and, always, death. She had put all her energy and

hope into that dance of recognition of strife, the real announcement of the beginning of months of violence, sudden death, the
conscription of youths into the emergency forces, the closing of
schools, terror, and insecurity. War.

There followed many more promises of recognition, soldiers,
weapons, peace, food; promises of a return to normalcy and a familiar world.

The promises were ultimately realized (even a war of attri-
tion must one day come to an end); the war ended, leaving people to find their healing and internal resolutions the best ways
they could.

"Camwood" reveals the crumbling of cultural and ritual stability. Unheard-of incidents happen and taboos are broken; the
moral stability of society is breached. In this tale, a nubile young
woman in the seclusion chamber in preparation for marriage is
virtually raped by a prospective suitor who turns out to be her
brother. Her dreams are blighted and hopes for a future are
stunted; the prevailing atmosphere of war affects everything
adversely. The tragic entanglement eventually costs the nubile
her life. The innocent and the guilty are leveled under the
hammer of an all-destructive fate.

In the eponymous "Broken Lives," the war has put intolera-
ble pressure on the lives of ordinary people. Previously stable
families are broken, erstwhile loving and harmonious relationships are dissolved, primary ties are torn apart, and communal
stabilities are shattered. The foundations of society are being
dismantled. The story portrays the silent tragedies of simple
people. The lowly absorb their enormous pain with remark-
able stoicism and philosophical calm. These people are no con-
ventional heroes, but their fortitude in the midst of so much
suffering is a kind of heroism. "Children's Day" highlights the
impact of the war on children. Deprived of the protective guidance of father and mother, the children are abandoned to their
own designs. The insecurities affect them as profoundly as the

adults; their lives are scarred by the same fears, anxieties, and uncertainties; their hunger is as unassuaged; and their lives are exposed to the same precariousness—in fact, they die as readily as the adults, only a little faster. They experience the same emotional stress and nervousness, conditions that stem from the disruption of normalcy. It is obvious that their childhood has been compromised by the general victimization that has followed the war. Denied the luxury of being children, they are made to assume the role of adults. Remarkably they show an imaginative growth in resolving their problems, but they also succumb to the pressures, revealing their fragility.

In "Ogbanje Father" the psychosis of war is complicated and confounded by the problem of high infant mortality, the ogbanje (spirit-child) phenomenon, and communal land disputes, creating a fatalistic atmosphere in which mountebanks, religious charlatans, and faith healers flourish. Driven to desperation by loss and suffering, the afflicted seek salvation in the most unlikely places; reason is suspended and superstition reigns. The war exacerbates problems that in more settled times were easily rationalized and controlled.

"Relief Duty" addresses one of the most important aspects of the Biafran war, namely: the contribution made by humanitarian and religious organizations to the alleviation of the tragedy of the Biafran people. The Biafran tragedy was deepened by the Federal side's use of starvation as a weapon of warfare. Since Biafra was completely blockaded by land and sea, religious and humanitarian organizations that attempted to bring relief (food and medicine) to the Biafrans had to do so with cargo planes that flew at night to evade Federal air patrols. These planes, flown by brave pilots, had to run the gauntlet of the Federal fighter planes, which succeeded in shooting some of them down. What the Biafran war revealed was that the sight of thousands of children and noncombatants dying the slow, painful death of malnutrition revolted the conscience of the world. Out of that revulsion emerged the French humanitarian organization Médecins sans Frontières (Doctors Without Borders), which would spare no effort to ensure that the Biafran tragedy was never repeated anywhere else in the world.

In the mystical world of the Igbo within which these tales are set, warfare, bloodshed, and destruction of life and property cause metaphysical pollution. At the end of all wars, there must follow the ritual purification of the earth to render it again habitable and to restore stability and balance to the disturbed world. In "Osondu," my favorite story of the collection, there has been a massacre of noncombatants who have taken refuge in a forest clearing outside their villages. Women survivors of the massacre, helped by two young Biafran soldiers who are themselves survivors from a major Federal offensive, bury the exposed bodies of the slaughtered villagers. But before going back to their villages, they perform rituals of purification over the newly dug graves, thus honoring the dead, cleansing themselves, and reclaiming the world from the evil that had polluted it. This tale in a very symbolic way pays deserved tribute to the women of Biafra and their contribution to the war emergency. It recognizes their good sense, boldness, and resourcefulness, their unique position as the invisible bulwark of Biafran resistance and custodians of the spiritual endurance of the people.

The last story, "The Gift," links the life of the narrator, the gift-child Onyinye, to the essence of motherhood, community, home, and, ultimately, the motherland or the wider community of the nation-state. It ends on a note of optimism, transcending the tragedy of the moment in affirmation of a future of peace and concord. If a substantial lesson has been learned from these tales it is that a nation of the complexity and diversity of Nigeria has a better chance of survival through the application of the feminine principles of humaneness, fairness, and justice than through untrammeled masculinity and relentless pursuit of naked power. Whether the hope and optimism expressed in the last story is realized, or is indeed realizable, depends on whether the feminine principles condition the dominant philosophy of the Nigerian state or continue to be negated by the believers in the omnipotence of power.

A wise fellow once said, "Fiction is the soul of history," by which one may surmise a certain paradox in the perception of the essence and meaning of an event. The seamless and uncharted episodes of history leave the mind bewildered, if not entirely overwhelmed, by their nature and scope, whereas fiction—as life organized, controlled, and trimmed to definite points of emotive resonances—renders reality assimilable and directed to specific purposes and enrichments of the appreciative soul. Out of the chaos of historic factuality may be distilled, through fiction, ineluctable truths that can increase understanding and enrich the emotions. This is the boon of fiction. How does fiction transform the tragedy of historical experience, such as the Biafran War, into the emotive, nourishing truths of literature? The short answer is, through the magic of art and the transmuting genius of a talented artist. *Broken Lives* exemplifies this transforming capacity of art. It is storytelling at its best, full of subtlety and a nuanced exploration of the core issues of the Biafran tragedy. This collection has proved once again that the Biafran story remains a viable source of literary creativity as long as there are those for whom the telling of it continues to provide an outlet for coming to terms with one of the greatest tragedies of modern times.

EMMANUEL N. OBIECHINA
Cambridge, Massachusetts, 2002

Preface

For a long time after the end of the Nigeria-Biafra War, images of the crisis, lost lives, deferred dreams, and irretrievable childhoods kept my mind alert to changes in the political climate, conversational tones, and song cadences.

I was already aware of the possibilities of story when the war started. Storytelling was standard fare in the evening at home as I was growing up. Throughout elementary school I used to look forward to the last period on Fridays, when pupils from different backgrounds and ethnic groups would be called to the front of the classroom to tell a story. Throughout the war, as our lives adjusted to the violence around us, adults and children remembered those Friday afternoons as part of a lost and peaceful homeland. However, as the war progressed and the restrictions on our lives increased, sitting in a story-circle became almost taboo as the daily need to not die became a priority for adults and children alike.

Several years later, in a creative writing class taught by Professor Jay Clayton at the University of Wisconsin, Madison, I was gently prodded alive again by the eagerness with which my teacher and classmates listened to my war stories. Every now and then someone would ask if I had really witnessed the situations I narrated. I tried not to cry. As a result, my responses were short as I struggled to relearn the art of narrative performance.

The stories in this collection are neither biography nor history. They are fictional accounts of the war experiences of ordinary people on the Biafra side of the crisis. Many readers who experienced Biafra will recognize some of the themes and the songs, which were mostly sung without instrumental accompaniment because of noise ordinances imposed by air raids and constantly shifting war fronts.

These are composite stories of women, men, and children as they struggled to make sense of a broken world, which continued to crumble without help from even the war as it raged through the land, destroying the sacred, the secular, and the indifferent. They are the stories of ordinary people caught in the middle of events they did not fully understand but from which they were determined to come out alive, well, and sane. For the women, the determination to hold on to what the men who went to war left behind was often foiled when their hometowns or villages became war fronts. As children starved, they also learned that the worst thing in life was not hunger or the fear of death but lack of security as fathers became men who were missing in action and mothers who went looking for basic necessities like food and salt were stranded behind enemy lines. For everyone, the constant but confusing noises of machine-gun fire, shelling, air raids, Biafran-made *ogbu-n'igwe*, dead-quiet afternoons interrupted only by gunfire, saltless food, kwashior-kor, and food aid provided confusing contrasts that strained the imagination.

I do not claim here to have done justice to the experiences of those Nigerians who experienced these crises. There is no way of understanding war. It does not bring about peace for citizens. Whether one is a soldier or civilian, a war fought in one's homeland desecrates the future and compels individuals, groups, and nations to reappraise the meaning of survival. But a war never provides the means to end war.

Broken Lives and Other Stories

Independence

We were getting ready for Independence to come to our town. In the villages, people were learning new dances and songs. It was rumored that a new masquerade would come out on that day. In our town, Akasi-of-the-nineteen-villages, a new dance is not unusual. But a new masquerade comes out only once in many generations.

At school we were told over and over that our uniforms had to be washed and ironed for March Past. My mother sent me with Elebuo to the stream. She told us to go in the morning, but as usual we waited until the sun was almost overhead. So when we arrived at the stream there was no one there. Not even a bird was chirping when we arrived at the big clearing before you turn the corner and see the water. But it was a beautiful hot day made for splashing around and swimming at the stream. It was a day made for feeling the world's knowing that you are there and that it expects your every move. Some of the rocks, the washing stones, poked their heads over the top of the water in the middle of the stream where the water was shallow. As usual, the water was so clear I could see every pebble in the streambed. On busy days, women, girls, men, and boys lined the stream's bank, pounding their dirty clothes on the washing stones. Others swam or splashed around in the deeper parts, while some sat on the bigger rocks, chatting, squabbling, gossiping.

Since I had not yet learned to swim, I liked to sit on one of the stepping-stones which form the path across the shallowest part of the stream. Although I got my bottom and my dress wet, it was a good place to sit and watch the rest of the stream, especially the deep part, where I am forbidden to go. From here, too, I would call out greetings to people walking across on the log bridge further up, near the place where you dip a waterpot, enamel basin, or bucket for drinking water. No one takes baths or washes clothes at the dipping pool. The water there is always cool, clean, refreshing, and sweet. Peaceful. The stones at the dipping pool are washed and the streambed cleaned twice a year by the newly married women.

Today, the day before Independence, I am here to wash my school uniform and splash around a little in the stream before fetching some water in my shiny new bucket. But when Elebuo and I arrived at the stream, it was quiet. I knew that Elebuo was disappointed too because she said sharply, "Nwada, remember— we can't swim without company. We will only wash the clothes and our uniforms." But I did not want to quarrel with her. I put my shiny new bucket on the ground and tried to sit inside it. Elebuo said I should not do that because girls do not sit like that. She likes to tell me how to do everything. Sometimes I don't even listen to her because I know she is not yet a woman.

Elebuo's light-blue enamel basin is full of dirty clothes. We are going to spend a long time at the stream. Tomorrow's parade will be the parade to end all parades. After tomorrow, we will never again march briskly past the British flag. Soon, I begin to march up and down the clearing, showing Elebuo how our class had practiced for March Past the day before. Every year school-children from all over the district march to the rhythms of school bands. March Past takes place in the big field in front of the district courthouse. Everyone says that after Independence comes we will never again march past the rainbow-canopied stand, listening intently for P. E. Master's command, "E-e-eyes right!"

My mother tells us that when they were children, they would march up and down the carefully tended paths that mark the boundaries of the schoolyard. Each teacher taught his or her class the marching steps before giving the children over to P. E. Master for the final selection. Nothing had changed since then. Every year the teachers still take the children out of class and drill them for hours in the hot sun for Empire Day. Elebuo tells me to be quiet because she knows all the March Past stories already, but I keep talking because I do not like the silence at the stream.

Last year, the year I started school, I went to the March Past. We marched to the rhythms of old and new marching songs. Some of them were tunes of Empire Day. Others had been made up over the years and I had learned them long before I joined the ABC class. My favorite song is the one about our country, and we marched to it yesterday. One of my cousins told me what the words mean because I do not understand or speak English very well. When the teacher was not looking, we did little dance steps to its rhythms, raising the red dust in each other's faces. Tickled by the warm dust, our bare feet could hardly match the rhythm of the song because they wanted to dance instead. Sometimes, we even played *oga* to the rhythms of the new song.

> Nigeria, the promised land.
> Africa, the great continent.
> We are marching on,
> To take our place,
> Among the great nations of the world!

Last year our teacher showed us how to salute the British flag. We had to hold our arms to our sides, maintain our marching steps, keep pace with each other, and stay in line until we passed the canopied stand. It was important that we start the salute long before we got to the stand. After that, P. E. Master would give the command, "E-e-eyes front!" That was the signal to swing our arms again. I was not interested in P. E. Master's details. I only wanted to be there when we won the trophy for St. Peter's Primary School in honor of the Queen.

This year, my happiness is endless because I have been chosen again among those to represent St. Peter's. The marching steps and the salute are still the same. Yesterday one of my uncles gave me a very nice haircut and my face looks new and shiny. My brother Nwankwo told me that I look like a newly hatched chicken.

"Keep quiet!" Elebuo is impatient. Although she knows the stories of March Past, I tell them to her all over again because I am worried about tomorrow.

"Stop that marching and come in the water and start washing your uniform or it will never get dry." Elebuo has already washed two or three of my mother's *lappas* and their matching blouses.

"You're going to cause that bucket to start leaking if you don't take care of it," Elebuo scolds as I drag my bucket through the sand and pebbles and step into the water. I take my dress from the bucket, careful not to drop the soap in the water. My mother always gives me a piece of Key Soap when I go to the stream. Today, my soap is wrapped carefully inside my uniform. I dip the dress in the water, then I press the soap to my nose. It is like no other smell I know, strange but clean. Elebuo is spreading some clothes on the grass. She moves from one spot to another, testing each one for dampness in the grass and gauging the sun's position. I am relieved when she does not cover the wildflowers with the wet clothes.

"Won't you come back into the water?" I ask Elebuo as I drip water from the wet uniform over my dry dress.

"Nwada, stop that!" Elebuo is angry because now I have to take a bath before we go home. "You're going to get yourself wet."

"But I like the way this water feels," I reply, squeezing more water down the front of my dress.

"Nwada! Stop it! You know your mother said that we should only swim if there are people at the stream. Listen, if you don't stop, the masquerade is going to catch you!" She knows that I am deathly afraid of masquerades. But I do not listen to her and I dip the dress once more into the water. Holding it over my head to smell the fresh, clean water. The sun looks like a cool, white fireball far away. When I am completely wet and cool, I spread the dress out on a washing stone and begin to rub the soap all over it.

"Gently, Nwada, gently! The stone will eat all your soap." Elebuo steps into the water, ready to take both dress and soap from me.

"It's my soap. My mother said I should wash this dress myself. She will iron it for me tonight."

"Hmmph! She didn't say you should finish the soap."

I stuck my tongue out at her.

"And don't be rude or I'll tell your mother."

Elebuo is one of my cousins. Although she is older and in Standard Three, we are good friends. Her mother is Father's younger sister, who came back from a bad husband. Her father lives far away in Ugwu Awusa, the Hausa highlands in the north. Now that they live with us, Elebuo also calls Father *Nna*, like my brothers and I. Sometimes she does errands for my mother. My mother likes her and Elebuo is like the sister I don't have.

Elebuo, my friend Maggie, and I do many things together. Today, Maggie could not come to the stream with us because she went to Uzoaro market with her mother. Yesterday we all helped fry the *garri* that they went to sell. This evening, when they come back from the market, we will go together to fetch water for the evening meal. Maggie is just a little bigger than me but she looks much taller. My mother says it's because of her long legs. She has beautiful dark brown skin, shiny and smooth like the shell of the *ugba* seed. She is the best oga player. Yesterday evening, when we were frying the garri, we talked about March Past. Everyone said that this year's should be different because Independence is coming.

Though I have been looking forward to the parade, I was worried because everyone was saying that this will be the only parade of its kind. I want our school to win again this year. Maggie's mother told me not to worry because we are marching for Independence. Independence is a good thing for us, she said.

But I do not understand this Independence. Everyone says that Independence is coming and that it is good. We children talk about it too. Who or what is it? Is it coming to visit? How long will she be here? Is she a relation of ours? Ours is a large family and it is possible to have a relation we have never met show up from a faraway place and be introduced as a close member of the family. Or, better still, someone we have been knowing all our lives would come to live with us and be explained within the context of our family. So, who is this Independence? My friend Maggie believes it is the end of the world that the priest talks about at church all the time. If that's so, Maggie and I have made plans about what to do. Maggie says she will run to a place so far away no one will ever find her. I won't run away because I do not want Independence to live in our town if we all leave. I will hide under Father's bed. I hid there once and no one was able to find me and neither will Independence. That way the world won't be able to end because I will still be here.

When I was younger, my parents, uncles, and older cousins used to talk about Independence. They said that we were not independent yet. They talked about Nkrumah, Zik, and others who were helping to find Independence. Sometimes it sounded as though Independence was something big and beautiful. Other times, it looked as if it could be one of the killing sins they talked about at church. Father said that the priest was not too happy about Independence. So, sometimes I think it must be bad for us to allow this Independence to come to our town. I ask Elebuo again, "Do you really know who Independence is?"

"I keep telling you it is a thing, not a person!" Elebuo does not look up from her washing.

"But how can it be a thing if it is coming to our town?"

"No, it is coming to the whole country."

"Is it very big, then? Where will it stay?"

"All over the country. Yes, it is big. Very big. People have been waiting for it for a long time. Here, help me wring this lappa." I hold one end of the lappa tightly while Elebuo wrings it until the water stops dripping. "If you listen to the speech tomorrow, you will understand. Our teacher says it is good to have Independence so we can rule ourselves."

I want to believe Elebuo and this Independence but I don't understand how it can be coming to our town and nobody knows where it will live yet we are getting ready for it.

"Who are its relations?"

"It doesn't have any. We're getting Independence from Britain!"

"Why? Do they not want it to stay in Britain?"

"No. It's something that they have over there which they give to people who want to rule themselves." It is obvious that I have said something to make Elebuo angry. I pound my blue dress hard against the stone, splattering soap bubbles and water all over my face and dress.

I cannot explain to Elebuo why I don't understand. I don't know how big the country is. Maybe it goes as far as Uzoaba, the town where Elebuo and her parents used to live before her father moved to Ugwu Awusa. We went there once. There the houses were too close together. Everyone had cars and bicycles and it was noisy and hot all the time. Maybe if Independence loses its way to Akasi and goes there instead, the nice priest would feel happy again about our country. Nne, my grandmother, says that all of us who go to the school on the hill will never learn anything. She says we are only going to bring trouble to the town. But she likes Independence because the old dances are coming back.

My father agrees with her sometimes. But not about Independence. I leave my dress and begin to imitate my father's talks about how we are not ready to rule ourselves. He doesn't believe that a young country like ours knows much about such things. He says Independence is the last thing on earth we will understand. Elebuo laughs. I do not know if she is laughing at me or at the things Nna says. I bend over my dress again, pounding, pounding on the stone. It will be here tomorrow.

Even the radio can't stop talking about it and the mammy wagons bring news of Independence every day. The women have a new hair style called Independence. A new kind of grass that grows fast covering every piece of earth it finds has been named the grass of Independence. I think Independence must be powerful and rich and some days I want to know her. I want her to hurry up and come to our town to show me why everyone talks about her all the time.

For the past few months the teachers have been telling us to remember to wash our uniforms for Independence Day. My mother told the seamstress to make a new one for me. My old one was a little tight and it had a little tear in it from the day I fell off the guava tree. But she finished it early so I already wore it to school for a week. She also had one made for my friend Maggie, who is not really my friend but her sister's daughter. Maggie has not worn hers yet. Everyone is getting ready for Independence to come to our town, to our school, and to the country.

People are learning new dances and songs. At school we have learned the new national anthem. Headmaster distributed little flags from big cartons to all the schoolchildren. The flags are green and white. My brothers and I placed our flags in our living room. When Father saw the four flags, he said that maybe Independence is not so bad after all. So he allowed us to go and watch the people learning new dances at the village square. Elebuo and I told my father again that we wanted to learn dances with one of the girls' groups. He said schoolchildren should not learn the dances of people who know nothing. But the dances of the know-nothing people are beautiful. Their songs remind me of the hills and valleys, Nne, and a full market on Afor days. If I could dance like that, I wouldn't mind if a hundred Independences came to our town. I would dance with my whole body, smiling like a person who knows no fear. But my father did not allow us to learn the dances of the know-nothing people, who stamp their feet to rhythms that will celebrate the unknown. Tomorrow.

Yesterday at school we marched to the sounds of the school band. The band played a tune that is popular this year.

> West African calypso.
> Nigerian independence.
> West Africa's biggest nation.
> Now we are independent.

We sang along with the band. The band played for us after march practice. We jumped up and down to the calypso tunes. We danced for a long time after the teachers left. We danced the new and special dances of Independence. I show Elebuo some of the steps in the water, splashing us both.

Elebuo says all the Independence songs will replace the Empire Day songs. I finish washing my uniform and spread it on the grass. Elebuo is still washing. She has already washed about five or six things and three sets of lappas to my one dress. I want to help her but she says I don't know how to wash older people's clothes. She tells me to sit down and rest or to take a bath in the shallow part of the stream, where she can see me.

I decide to take a bath. I spread my almost-dry dress on the grass and wade into the stream in my drawers. When I get tired of scooping the water up to my face at the shallow end of the stream, I wade a little deeper. Elebuo is talking about the easy and exciting life in Uzoaba township and how you don't need to go to the stream every day. So she doesn't notice that I am going away from the shallow end of the stream. The deeper I wade, the better the water feels to my warm skin. The water at the deeper end of the stream is cool and I am not afraid. I am now up to my chest in the water and I can no longer see the streambed clearly. Swimming is not going to be difficult. I stretch my arms out to swim.

"Did you hear what I said?" I haven't said anything for a while and she turns to see what I am doing. "Chineke! Nwada! Where are you going?" Her voice is afraid, a warning.

I turn around to look at her, smiling. But my scream pierces the warm afternoon as my feet lose touch with the streambed. The water swallows the rest of my scream and I splutter and thrash around, grasping for anything solid. But the earth is gone and there is water everywhere. Elebuo, who had come back to Akasi from a township with pipe-borne water, is screaming too. She cannot swim. She starts to run toward me but stops when the water gets too deep. I don't know what happened but somehow I am now floating on my back. I cannot move my arms or legs. The water is taking me away from Elebuo and I do not know how to turn myself around or over. Usually, I stay in the place where the water is only waist-deep. My screaming stops. Though I am too afraid to move my arms or legs, I am moving slowly downstream. I hear Elebuo's screams from far away as the silent stream carries me into the forest.

Just as I am giving myself up for a lifetime of floating on water to unknown and fearful places, my head hits something hard. It is a stone. I grab at it and my feet strike the streambed. Here, the stream is suddenly shallow as it bends its way through the forest. I stand up, panting and coughing. The branches hang low enough over the stream that the leaves touch my back and I shiver. Here, the sun does not come through the branches of the ancient trees. I walk to the edge of the stream, pressing each foot firmly into the streambed. I come to a path but I can no longer hear Elebuo's voice. I call her name.

"Where are you?" she replies.

"I'm here! I am coming! Where are you?" I am running toward her voice. Hot tears stream down my face, although I do not remember when I started to cry. As I come out from behind a big tree, I run straight into Elebuo. She embraces me and lifts me off the ground. Her tears fall hot on my shoulders and back. When we reach the open area of the stream, she begins to gather the clothes from the grass. She wipes my face with a warm wet lappa and hands me my dress. Then the words come, pitching the afternoon into the forest. Unaimed, her voice fills the valley and I feel the sun warm again on my back.

"Chineke nwannem! What would I have told your mother today? Nwada, why don't you ever listen? Chineke. Why was I not looking? But I know your ears are made of leather. What was I doing? I thought you were right there until I didn't hear you say anything about Independence. You who have spoken, eaten, and slept nothing but Independence for the past two months. Then I looked around just in time to see your head disappear under the water. Chineke is great. Both your *chi* and mine must be wide awake." She continues to admonish both of us, punctuating every statement with thanks to our chi and Chineke. She folds the clothes that are already dry into one pile, tying them inside a lappa. She does not even look at me when I suggest that we wait for everything to dry. Instead, she asks the question that has been worrying me all afternoon, "I wonder where the whole world has gone to this afternoon? Nobody heard me screaming for help."

The question brings back my fear. What if Independence had come and taken everyone while we were here at the stream? Maybe they forgot to come and call us back to the village to go with them. Maybe that was why we met everyone going up the hill earlier.

As I pull my dress over my head, I hear the muffled sound of masquerade drums and fling myself into Elebuo's arms. The masquerade grove is not too far away from the village. It is ru-mored that the grove is somewhere between our village and the stream. I cling to Elebuo, sobbing. I tell her I do not want to be left behind. If Independence has taken everyone away, I don't know what I will do. Elebuo tells me to stop. A foreigner to our hometown, she does not know what to do if the masquer-ades come to the stream. She promises to protect me from Independence.

"If Independence has taken everyone, I'll carry you on my back and we will walk all over until we find that Indepen-dence." She wades into the dipping pool. No one is allowed to wade in the dipping pool because it makes the drinking water dirty. But Elebuo wades in the pool because there is nobody to tell her not to and she wants to give me the cleanest water to take home. If anybody finds out, the women will make her clean the stream by herself and her mother will pay a fine. She fills my shiny new bucket and we start up the hill.

Elebuo does not say anything to me as I struggle to contain my excitement at finding the village intact. My brother Nwan-kwo and some boys are playing soccer at the village square. People call out greetings. No one mentions Independence but I know that it will be here tomorrow.

After Elebuo spread the clothes out to dry, she went and told my mother about what happened at the stream. My mother was very angry and started to tell the whole world how my ears were made of cowhide and I had come to this world to show her some sense. She called on her chi, asking why all she could give her was this one daughter who was determined to expose them both. As soon as I found a gap in the string of questions that my mother reserves for her chi and Chineke, I slipped away to Elebuo's house, where my aunt fussed over me for the rest of the afternoon.

That evening, my parents treated me as if I had just come back from a long journey. They smiled and spoke to me in low, gentle tones. After the evening meal, Grandfather poured some palm wine on the ground near the front door and thanked the ancestors for giving them another chance with the *ogbanje*. As I watched him pour the libation, I wondered if the earth likes palm wine and when I would be old enough to drink some myself. Only my brother Nwankwo scolded me when he heard what happened.

"Why are you always getting into trouble?" he asked me. "Do you want to die?"

"You can go and die yourself if you want to," I flashed back at him. "You're just looking for my trouble."

"But why were you trying to drown yourself?"

"I was not! Leave me alone!" I was angry. I didn't think about it as drowning until he said that. I went to the kitchen to help my mother. She was sorting small stones from rice in a large tray. When I went to sleep, my mother was still cooking the rice-and-stew, our lunch after the March Past.

I woke up several times to the sound of drums. The dancers were putting final touches to their dance steps. I tried not to think of the new masquerade.

In the morning, my uniform was ironed and draped over a chair in the living room. I took a quick bath behind the kitchen and bolted down my breakfast of hot boiled yam with seasoned palm oil. My brothers looked handsome in their khaki shorts and white shirts. Later, Elebuo and my friend Maggie came and we left together on the long walk to the district courthouse in Uzoaro. P. E. Master inspected us, sending a few students with unsatisfactory uniforms into the waiting crowd. Our line formed and we marked time, waiting our turn to march down the field.

Soon the band struck up our school song and after a few false starts we fell into step and marched toward the rainbow-canopied stand. As we approached the stand, I noticed that the district commissioner was not taking the salute to Independence. The flag of Independence was green and white and new, like the small ones Headmaster gave us at school.

P. E. Master was decked out in his scout master's khaki uniform, a large yellow handkerchief around his starched collar. Good-natured and energetic, he seemed made for the job. He marched up and down the line, swinging the baton to his chant: "Lef-tright! Lef-tright! Lef-tright!" I was swinging my arms, looking straight ahead and keeping the pace, when I felt my stomach bump into the back of the person in front. At the same time, someone bumped into my back. P. E. Master ran back to our end of the line as we tried to steady ourselves and regain the pace. Meanwhile, the command, "E-e-eyes right!" was given at the front of the line. Later someone said one of the younger schoolchildren had stubbed a toe against something in the grass. The command was given by one of the senior pupils when those in front realized that something had gone wrong with the original plan. Crooked and ragged, our end of the line continued to march, our hands to our sides, faces turned right in our salute to the new flag.

The man at the stand looked very important in his dark suit. He received our salute, his right hand held just so, like the DC's last year. We had almost reached our school sign when P. E. Master remembered to say, "E-e-eyes front!" We took our place, standing in line behind the sign. From here, we had to jump up and down or stand on each other's shoulders to see the rainbow-canopied stand. But the teachers told us to stop, promising severe punishment to those who persisted.

After the March Past, the speeches started. All the speeches were in English and it was difficult to keep the schoolchildren in their places in the hot sun. Boy Scouts immediately set up a

rope barrier, threatening everyone with sticks that material-
ized from nowhere.

Had I been able to fully understand the language, I would
not have understood what was said because I did not hear
most of it. Elebuo interpreted what she could hear for me. All
the speakers talked about the glory and joy of self-rule.

Soon even those who understood the language could not
tell us much, as the noise from the spectators increased. Dancers
walked about in their colorful costumes, jingling ankle bells
and rattles in a cacophony that steered the crowd toward a different language and form. People were eager for the perfor-
mances to begin. Even the dignitaries at the canopied stand
were leaving their seats. I wished I could go to the canopied
stand for protection from the searing sun or find a drink of
cool water. But, as schoolchildren, our respects to Independence included waiting for all the speeches to finish.

Although our school did not win the marching trophy, it was
a sweet day. My brothers and I ate our rice-and-stew lunch.
Then we went to see the new masquerade. It was a different
kind of masquerade. The dancers were fast and agile. Their
calling songs had a few words of pidgin English. Unlike the
usual masqueraders, they were not aloof and dignified. They
talked back at people, seeming not to know the boundaries between the world of spirits and the rest of us. When it looked
like they were going to become violent, some of the older men
in the crowd called them off the improvised arena.

It was frightening to see masquerades lose control of the
spirit dance and agree to be treated like real people. The older
men did not seize their masks but led them away with ancient
calls and songs of older masquerades. We did not see them
again until later, and they were not dancing.

There were many different kinds of dances. Some were old.
Many were new. Older men's and women's dances were slow
and flowing, soothing the spirit after the encounter with the

new masquerade. Fast youth dances raised the tempo to the rhythms of unseen tomorrows. Elebuo, my friend Maggie, and I spent our three-penny allowances on *akara* and ash-roasted, salted groundnuts. The women admired our uniforms and told us how well we had marched.

On the way home, we fought with the children from the school who had won the trophy. Rolling in the red dust and screaming at the top of our voices, it was more of a game than a fight, for we were all related by blood or marriage. Though we went to different schools and churches, we could not forget the long-standing ties necessary for our existence.

By the time we arrived home we were dirty and tired. Elebuo, my friend Maggie, and I went to the stream to wash ourselves and fetch some water for the evening meal. As we came up the hill, we came face-to-face with the young men, the dancers of the new masquerade. Still wearing their raffia skirts, they were going to the stream to wash off the charcoal and sweat. One of them held a fearful mask under his arm. Maggie, who was walking in front, stopped. For a long minute, neither ourselves nor the young men spoke. Then one of them laughed the guttural laughter of the spirit world.

"These are the schoolchildren who were laughing at us at the field," said another.

"Leave them alone," said one. "They are schoolchildren and do not understand."

"Let's teach them what they don't know, then," said the one with the mask.

"I said, leave them alone."

There was nowhere for us to turn. The path to the stream is not narrow but it is banked by high walls scraped out of the red earth. The ancient tree branches have been trimmed and tended over the years to provide natural shade all the way to the stream. I have always felt safe in this cool, wide, red tunnel with its roof of ancient branches.

The young men spread out, blocking our way up the hill. I noticed the clean hoe marks on the red earth wall as if for the first time. Here and there new moss and grass were growing back. Some of the moss near the tree roots had been missed by the hoe many times and was a darker green.

"We are going to show you how to run off and be school-children," said one of the young men.

"Yes. We will show you how to laugh at masqueraders." They were almost on top of us. They stood around us, some slightly above us, compelling us to show our fear. I was trembling.

"Is this little one a schoolchild too?" asked the one with the mask. His laughter brought bile to my throat.

"Yes. And your mother sent me," I flung back at him even as Elebuo hastened to cover my mouth. The next few minutes were a flash of lightning. He reached out with his leg, hooking it behind mine. I slipped. My new bucket went tumbling down the rocky hillside as if it had a life of its own. Its clattering sounded like distant laughter echoing through the hills and forest. Almost with a single motion, Maggie and Elebuo threw the water in their enamel basins at the two youths nearest them.

"Nwada! Run!" We ran back toward the stream screaming at the top of our voices.

"My father! My mother! Help! Help! Masqueraders! Ma-a-asqueraders-are-after-us!"

They chased us, threatening to do all kinds of harm if they caught us. As we neared the stream, some men came running from the wine tapper's shed. The young men saw them and ran back up the hill. The men tried to calm us down and helped us to find our bucket and basins. When we found my bucket, it was knocked out of shape. But except for some scrapes and bruises, none of us was hurt. The men told us to forget the water for the evening meal and go home. They walked with us as far as the village playground. Later they would come to tell our parents what they knew.

Maggie and Elebuo went home with me. We stayed up late telling and retelling the events of the day. I had almost drifted off to sleep when Maggie said into the darkness, "Nwada, are you awake?"

"Yes," I said.

"Did you see that Independence?"

"No."

"Maybe it was hiding."

"Do you think it will come before morning?"

"What do you mean?"

"I am saying that the grown-ups may be wrong. Independence might be the end of the world after all."

I started to cry. My mother came into the room. "What is it?" she said.

"I don't want to die."

"What are you talking about? Who said you are going to die?"

"Maggie said that Independence is the end of the world, and I don't want the world to end."

"It won't. Now, go to sleep."

Maggie was sniffling too. Elebuo said nothing.

"Stop that and go to sleep, both of you." My mother went to bring the hurricane lamp.

"Nkemjika! What is it?" Nna called into the night.

"Nothing. It's these children and their talk about Independence. They think it's the end of the world." Her voice was coming to us from far away. It sounded like it was coming from a far and dark place.

"Maybe they are right," Father replied. "Maybe this Independence is the end of the world." Mama came back into the room with the lamp. She turned down the flame and sat on the bed. We told her again about the March Past and Independence Day and the young men and their new masquerade. I could not fall asleep for a long time. Each time I closed my eyes, I saw the young man with the fearful mask under his arm. My mother must have sat there until I fell asleep because when I woke up later, the lamp was still there and she was gone. I slept uneasily that night, waking up many times. I was afraid that Independence would come and carry us all into the unknown.

Angelus

The bell ringer finally tolled the Angelus. We had been waiting for that sound all day. Reverend Mother Principal had promised that it would signal the end of classes for the day. We were going to have a lesson on air raids and how to protect ourselves in the unlikely event of an attack. Excited about the rare event of ending classes at midday, we stumbled over the familiar words of the Angelus. Excitement made our tongues clumsy, our prayers incoherent.

"Holy Mother, Mary of Grace, pray f'rus . . ." Someone giggled.

Mother Mary H. glowered at us. She did not know whether to punish us right away, deal with us later, or let us go unpunished for once. We continued praying, watching her mobile face and expressive blue eyes.

"That we may be made worthy . . ." We could already hear girl voices outside mixed with the last solemn strokes of the bell. We rushed onto the big lawn as soon as we finished reciting the troublesome Angelus. Mother Mary H. did not punish us that afternoon.

Ours was a class of teenagers in training to become "properly educated young women and leaders of tomorrow" at this exclusive secondary school for girls planted in the eastern part of Obodo by the Catholic mission. The school grounds were beautifully kept, their big green lawns marked with large gray buildings held in place with arches and columns. The clean concrete pathways directed residents as well as visitors from one building to another. Students said, half jokingly, that no one could ever get lost at Our Lady of Peace Secondary School for Girls. Each of the paths led to a viable destination on the school premises. There was really nowhere else to go except to a classroom, a dormitory building, or any of the many functional, red-roofed concrete buildings. The farthest reaches of the school grounds were carefully marked with a barbed-wire fence that students seldom tried to scale or crawl under.

Our Lady of Peace School for Girls was not a very big school. School history said that it was built on the dreams of a wealthy young nun from faraway England. Born into wealth, she wanted an idyllic setting from which she would do the work of her God. Her people, wanting her to enjoy the fruits of their labor, gave the mission some money for this ravishingly beautiful property on a hill about two miles from the nearest village. According to the story, this piece of earth had been fallow for many generations because the people of nearby Ikot Nyin village, whose land it was, said the land was cursed. What or who had cursed the land varied depending on who told the story. The villagers said that long ago this piece of land was an evil forest where people who had committed abominations were left to die. But mission history said that long ago, people who were kidnapped were hidden there to await transportation to the coast. Whatever the truth, no buildings had ever been built on this land, and no man or woman had cultivated anything on it for generations.

After the mission got the land, the villagers refused to have anything to do with anything built on the cursed hill. For many years the mission wanted to build a church on the land. It would be a brick building, the biggest church in this part of Obodo. People would come from far and near to worship in it. But the villagers said they would not set foot in the church. Converted or not, they were not going to confront the evil spirits of their land on purpose. Finally, the bishop ordered the work to begin. It would be the biggest brick church building in the area. Builders were brought in from other parts of Obodo. When the builders heard about the curse, they built a small mud house instead and ran off with what little money they had been paid. A few weeks after they left, the mud church building was struck by lightning. Angry villagers razed what was left of it to the ground. Soon after, the bishop fell sick and had to go back to England. Another one was promptly sent in his place. While the second bishop was still trying to understand the lore of the mission in this part of Obodo, the wealthy young nun made the offer to the mission with her family's support. The nun's gift solved the problem. The new bishop agreed to build a secondary school for girls, and the wealthy young nun became the first principal of Our Lady of Peace Secondary School for Girls. She served the school for fifteen years before returning to her homeland.

That was before our time. Visible proof of her presence and work at Our Lady's was preserved in Assembly Hall. There everyone could see the beautiful picture of the Mother in a white dress and gray wimple. In the picture, her smile was gentle and her brown eyes followed you everywhere.

Our Lady's school admitted students from all over the country and beyond. But the villagers of Ikot Nyin remained aloof, refusing to have a hand in the mission's solution of luring unsuspecting girls from all over the country into cursed and forbidden ground. As it turned out, the land was fertile and everything planted or thrown on it grew, including young girls. The nuns tended the girls on their own, using a brand of love familiar only to them mixed with strong doses of religion, mathematics, English language and literature, and other exciting subjects. With the help of a few paid local gardeners, the nuns planted and tended flowerbeds of violets, hibiscus, canna lilies, bachelor's buttons, and many other blossoms, local and imported. The school gardens were so beautiful that every Visiting Sunday, people came from all over Obodo to admire them. The nuns charged the visitors donations for the upkeep of the school. In return, the visitors received nicely clipped violets, hibiscus, canna lilies, bachelor's buttons or other flowers in season.

The day of the air raids lesson, Mother H. was having difficulty acting the part of role model for the energetic Obodo girls she had taken under her wings as part of her vow to serve her God. For our part, we found her fascinating. Her real name was Reverend Mother Mary Rosemary. But some of the more daring senior girls called her Mother Rose. She was our classmistress and we called her Mother Mary Hibiscus because we thought the hibiscus flower was a more fitting namesake for a nun in an African girls' school. Besides, there were more hibiscus flowers than roses on the school premises.

This time of year, the lawn stretched dark green and thick and, every day, students were punished for walking on its lush, cool greenness. That afternoon, students not only walked on it, they ran on the thick, soft, green carpet. Some girls even sat down on the grass, although our heavily starched deep-blue box-pleated skirts were supposed to remain immaculately clean all week. But it was a special day and no prefect or teacher said anything. For once, grass stains on our clothes did not matter. Besides, nobody seemed to know what this special speech was about. All we knew was that Obodo was already in crisis. A State of Emergency had been declared and all the students who came from outside the boundaries of our great Obodo were airlifted the week before back to their home countries in other parts of the continent. There were rumors that the school would close and that everyone would have to go back to their hometown.

The State of Emergency caused some of the senior girls to begin to read their history books more closely. They took more careful notes on details of the world wars, the Hundred Years' War, and all other such wars. They looked for real-life issues in those foreign wars that up until two months before were only points to be scored in the biweekly tests. They looked for details of what girls did during wars. So far no one had been able to determine what young women did beyond the glossed-over information about rape and plunder. Every night, after lights-out, the older girls talked about history and war in far-away places. They spoke about King Arthur and his knights; did anyone know if they were real or not? They discussed real historical figures like King George and Queen Victoria, Joan of Arc, and Queen Mary, and people in faraway countries where men fought duels to defend their honor, their ladyloves, or the lives of beloved family members. They argued about the thundering hooves of horses going to war, men marching for miles through enchanted forests, and dangerous river crossings in the dead of winter. They dreamed of forts, castles, and coats of armor and knights who fought with swords and lances and accomplished deeds of valor for home and country. They wondered where the world wars were fought and why, if they were world wars, they did not feature in local war stories. Those who knew said that local men who were drafted into the African end of the Second World War had gone to faraway countries to fight.

We laughed shyly about the River Niger and the Benue, which had never drowned any knights because they had no forts or castles built near them. We worried about rape and plunder, unable to decide what it would feel like to be in a war in a country without castles or forts. Rape we could understand. Maybe there would be many men. Maybe only a few men or one. But what was there to plunder? Besides, it was difficult to decide what the English words meant in nothing-to-plunder African places without kings, serfs, or fjords. Places that had only unknown, unmapped towns, rivers, and hills. Tropical African villages whose men did not have knightly traditions and whose ancestors were familiar only with ancient sacrifices of eggs and little yams and chicken feathers. The English literature experts talked about "the rape of the lock" and decided that as African girls, without magnificently beautiful heads of hair, we did not qualify for that kind of rape. It did not occur to us that because as young women living in the crevices of cultures in conflict, we did not qualify for a real-life understanding of rape of any kind. Yet.

Our early and daily training on leadership was given us by teachers who forgot to tell us that African independence was a consequence of the sweat, tears, and blood of our younger and educated elders and was still under discussion. Although we loved them and sang praise songs about their achievements, we did not yet know that Nkrumah, Azikiwe, and Kenyatta were heroes worth emulating. We did not yet understand that Mount Kenya, the Zambezi River, the Senegal, and the Congo were ours and were depending on us to continue to keep them safe from harm. We did not know that our country had already been raped and that our parents sent us to Our Lady of Peace to learn how to help them help us deal with the pain which that knowledge was sure to bring.

Our split knowledge of history allowed us to be comfortable discussing other people's struggles for independence and free-dom but not with Obodo's past, current, or future aspirations. Each of us knew our ancestral past in ways that gave us confidence and the ability to rise to the variety of situations created by the nuns who were training us to lead our nation into a star-studded future. But the nuns also forgot to teach us to build on our wealth of knowledge of the things that had kept our ancestral lands sacred and vibrant. The wealthy nun with the intense brown eyes whose picture graced Assembly Hall was our new ancestor. Her eyes following us around the school premises ensured our safety, and our loyalty to the school and its new traditions would guide us to her vision.

That day at Our Lady of Peace, with no idea of how big or small this State of Emergency was, we waited, hopeful, as we played on the lawn. Some of the bigger girls already had an idea of what to expect from the lesson on air raids. They had heard about this new event from the students at our brother school, St. Michael's School for Boys, when they went there the previous weekend for a debate on the merits and demerits of polygamy. The boys had told them that it was nothing to worry about. We waited.

Beyond the school fences, the surrounding hills and valleys blazed with the colors of trees in bloom. Far away in the township, the aluminum roofs blinked their response to the afternoon sun.

All week students had rumored that taking cover meant throwing yourself on the ground, facedown, as soon as an airplane was sighted. Some said you did not have to see it; you only had to hear it and then, *fiam!* like lightning, you had to run outside and throw yourself on a soft bed of grass. No one knew what to do if there was no lawn with cool, thick, evenly cut green grass. The day before, during Games Period, our class spent some time worrying about the idea of "Take cover!" Some thought that only enemy planes were suspect. Others said that all planes were now suspect and that you had to do the lightning run each time an airplane flew by.

Velvet, my neighbor in the dormitory, said it was going to be difficult since our school was near the airport. We might just as well make our beds on the lawn, as we would be running to take cover on it all day, she said. She acted like an encyclopedia on air raids all week simply because some soldier uncle of hers had told her some things about air raids when she went home for her cousin's church wedding two weeks before.

But Velvet usually knows how these things work. So we listened, enthralled by her accounts. She comes from a very large family and there are experts of all kinds among her many

cousins, aunts and uncles. Velvet is pretty, with coal-black skin
that shines. Some of the girls always remind her that she has
the pleasing dark skin of people from Ghana or Senegal. Her
teeth are even and white like well-washed *egusi* seeds. The only
thing I don't like about Velvet is that she talks all the time.
With Velvet as my neighbor in the dormitory, it's difficult to
get a word in, and that can be annoying if you also like to talk.

On the netball court that evening, no one could say anything
that Velvet did not already know. But this time we all thought
she was adding a little salt and pepper to the truth when she
said people could die from "Take cover!" Our class, Form Two
A, was supposed to play a match against Form Two B. We
ended up pretending to take cover from the ball as people
caught and threw it at one another for the rest of the hour.
When the bell rang for Refectory, we were still not sure what
to expect for the next day. But our ignorance on the subject of
"Take cover!" was nothing compared to the fact that we did
not have a Games Period report to give to Mother H. the
following morning. As it turned out, on the day of the "Take
Cover!" speech, with classes over early, we didn't have to give the
report. We planned two matches later so we would give Mother
H. a double report the following day. It would be difficult to
fool her. But it was a challenge making the plans because we
knew she always expected us to try and stay ahead of her.

I liked Mother H. It was always a challenge trying to guess
what turn a conversation with her was going to take. She was
one of those women of God who took their work seriously. These
women from distant lands who had chosen the task of turning
generations of teenage African girls into Proper Young Women,
Leaders of Tomorrow. Mother H. never lost an opportunity to
remind us of their goals for us. It was difficult to decide whether
she really liked us or whether we were only a part of the fulfill-
ment of her vows to the god of her ancestors. Sometimes Mother
H. reminded me of my aunt, my father's oldest sister, who is a

leader of the women in my village, Oboroji in Akasi-of-the-
nineteen-villages. Both women spoke of the same things. About
being woman, and . . . all that. But there the comparison ended.

My aunt was a leader of women in a way that reminded me
of the bright sun and the rolling hills of my hometown. She
had firmly refused to be educated in the new and foreign ways,
preferring instead to work with my grandmother to provide a
way for my father, who was fascinated with the new ways from
the start. With their hard work, he achieved his goals in education and was the assistant director of a new trading company whose headquarters were in England. He hoped to go to
England one day. My aunt's ambitions never changed. She was
firm of voice and step, and you always knew when she was
pleased or angry. Her place was in the village, close to the ancestors and the people.

I haven't decided what it was about Mother H. that blurred
the comparisons I was always trying to find or make between
her and my aunt. It wasn't that Mother H. walked fast, making
no sound whatsoever on the concrete floors of the classroom,
chapel, or refectory. Nor was it that one minute she was not in
the room while the very next minute she would be in the
middle of a conversation you were having with a friend. Her
interjections into our conversations made us feel unsafe in a safe
kind of way. She was our mathematics teacher and her love for
her subject and the teaching profession made it difficult to believe the other things she said about the version of the Proper
Woman that she and her colleagues in their white costumes
and cloth masks taught us at Assembly, in class, or in Chapel.

It was probably the fact that when Mother H. taught mathematics, there was a glint in her eyes that defied all that talk
about propriety and womanhood. My aunt had a similar glint
in her eyes when she talked about the market at the end of the
day. How she and her friends had kept the prices from falling
to unreasonable lows despite the fact that the traders from the

township markets had brought their troublemaking, haggling selves. I spend a great deal of time with my aunt. She lives in a nearby compound, where she is the first wife of the wealthy and generous Eze-ji. Her husband's barns are always full of yams and he has taken the *Nde-ji* title reserved for the strongest and wealthiest yam planters in the area. I like yams and since she always has cooked yam in her kitchen, I spend a significant portion of the day at my aunt's house. During my countless visits, she is often in conversation with one or the other woman. They talk about market prices, proper social conduct, so-and-so's coming out ceremony, how someone was trying to act like the best wife in the world, or how someone else was ruining the name of women in the town due to her unsatis-factory upbringing. Sometimes she worried about my Aunt Ejituru's third daughter's rights as the second wife of her hus-band in nearby Eleoha village or how some young woman in Umuiwe was likely to die from a pregnancy that did not sit well on her. As I grew older, she sometimes took me with her to the farm and the conversations and stories would continue all day long between my aunt and her friends. Except for a few occasions, I never knew how or when the women solved the ever-present problems. But I never saw the glint leave my aunt's eyes and she never gave up.

During mathematics class, Mother H. reminded me even more of my aunt, her blue eyes dancing at the chance to show us how *a* did not equal *b*, how sometimes one would be greater than the other. I was always intrigued by the wily nature of the foreign letters in mathematics class and could never get them to apply to anything else in my life. During those moments of conflict between my elemental, primitive knowledge of things that did not match and my instinctive understanding of shifty roman alphabets next to arabic numerals in mathematics classes, I had difficulty believing the gestalt that formed my aunt and my teacher. This difficulty may also have had to do with the fact that most days I ended up on the veranda outside the class-room with the predictable punishment of emptying a five-gallon bucket of water with a teaspoon, spoon by spoon, for daydreaming. Always within earshot of the class and Mother H.'s watchful eyes, I listened to the lessons and remained the top student in mathematics in my class. Beyond that, I was the class jester. Some days, she would order me to stand on one leg in the corner of the classroom, my little finger pointing at a chalk spot marked on the floor. If I was in a good mood, I would topple over every so often, landing in a heap in the cor-ner and setting the class off into girlish giggles. On other days I cried, wetting the floor with hot tears until Mother H. had mercy and sent me back to my desk.

"Daydreaming again, Nwanyieze? Here's Mother H.!" Grace interrupted my thoughts. I did not hear her come and sit next to me on the grass. Girls milled around us in the hot lazy afternoon.

"I already emptied the bucket today," I said with a smile.

"That's probably why your head is empty," she retorted. "You should stay away from those women. They are from distant lands and do not understand people who have *agwu*, like you. What are you thinking about?" She arranged her pleats into neat rows down her outstretched legs.

"Stop it. I do not have *agwu*. I'm an ordinary person."

"That's what they all say. Do you know when this event will start?" she waved her hand in a circular motion to include all the people on the lawn.

"No. But I hope the speaker will be here soon. This sun is killing me."

"Yes, and you predicted rain this morning." Grace looked into the blazing sky, which seemed to be burning up in its own heat. She had laughter in her eyes.

"Well, that tells you how much of my *agwu* is working," I laughed back at her.

Grace was easily the prettiest girl in our class. Her uniform was always clean and neat against her smooth, dark skin. Next to her, I looked every inch the teenager we both were, while she looked the perfect picture of Mother H.'s Proper Woman. We hailed from the same part of the country and were best friends. Our classmates called us David and Goliath because we were so different from each other and they could not understand how we could be such good friends.

The conversations around us merged into a soothing market-like drone, blanketing us in a cocoon of privacy rarely found at Our Lady's school for girls. The prefects seemed off-duty and there were no teachers in sight. Although the sun was hot, it was a rare opportunity to be out here in the middle of the day and the break from the backbreaking routine of classes, prayers, games, more classes, and more prayers was good. Everything in our lives was highly organized in this all-girls boarding school. Situated on a hill far away from the nearest town, we needed special permission to leave the school premises on any pretext. All our needs could be bought or given to us on pre-paid tabs at the one-room general store that was run by the women of God and managed by the school prefects.

We enjoyed the privilege of being set apart from other girls who could not afford to be here either because their parents would not let them go to a Catholic mission school or because they did not have the means. In our circles, elitism was not only encouraged, it was a requirement. The nuns required it; we reveled in it. The nuns managed our admission and subsequent membership in this new world that they were creating through education. Either we did not see it or we refused to recognize the leveling of social classes that our uniforms evoked. Here we could not strive for distinction on the bases of the norms and rules excerpted from our different and various ancestral backgrounds. Here, everything we owned was always and already stipulated on the prospectus that each student received with the acceptance letter from Our Lady of Peace Secondary School for Girls. From the enamel buckets we used to take our cold baths at five o'clock every morning to the brown Bata sandals that made up our daily uniforms, every single girl owned the same set of things. It did not matter whether you were a first-year student or in Upper Six, you were not allowed any privileges except those that students made up on their own outside the school rules. The only thing that differed was our names. Sometimes, even that was not guaranteed, as most of the students had taken new names at baptism or conversion into the variety of Christian denominations that dominated our lives.

On Sundays we wore white dresses with wide sashes tied in neat bows at the back, our heads covered with pink Mother Goose bonnets that we made in our very first needlework class.

As teenagers, we loved the living away from home for the first time, and the friendships were close. The annual meetings and activities of the Old Girls' Association hinted at the lifelong nature of the friendships we were forming. Security looked us in the face and we beamed back. Our days were measured and full. We were happy. We were the promise that had been made to our great, great-grandparents at colonization. We were Africa's future. We waited.

Maybe this day would show us the extent of that promise. We waited. We waited for the speech that would teach us how to be safe from air raids, how to take cover from sudden but planned attacks from the vast skies of our homeland and from the large expanse of our hope-filled lives and futures. The sun blazed the same message it had given to our ancestors but we paid no attention, feeling only its heat.

Gradually, the buzz of conversation began to die down. People were turning toward the study hall. A tall man in a black suit was walking toward us. Reverend Mother Principal was with him. A sigh of disappointment swept through the crowd of waiting young women. We were expecting an army officer in uniform, a real soldier.

A whisper went around, "It's an army officer. He's in mufti."

The nun and the man in the suit walked up to the edge of the lawn and waited for the silence that would accompany our acknowledgment of their presence. The rest of the teachers came out to the veranda of the study hall building. Someone finally jingled a bell for silence.

"Good afternoon," said the tall suit in a bright, official voice. His copper-bronze skin glistened with sweat in the hot sun. It was difficult to tell if Mother Principal was sweating. Covered from head to toe in her shining white attire, only a little bit of her face and hands could be seen. Unlike the *ekpo* masquerade in my hometown, she managed to inspire awe and fear without running or dancing to the music of her ancestors. A strikingly different kind of masquerade, she had taught us to stand in place with an unnamed fear of a ritual that evoked itself in stationary symbols whose unblending solid colors silenced the flamboyance of our tropical homeland.

From far away I heard what the army officer was saying. He was part of a team that was preparing young people like us for the crisis that had already started. His name was Col. George Something-or-Other. I couldn't hear his last name. His speech was crisp, his pace fast. He talked about taking cover and how we must remain good citizens. This war would soon be over, he said. Just a question of months. For now we should remember to take cover during air raids. The pilots had been warned not to drop bombs on civilians, and the soldiers would take care of the people. This visit was just a formality. A just-in-case kind of thing, you know. As young people, we should continue to study. Our education was important. Reverend Mother Principal would tell us what to do at all times and we should obey her and our teachers. At the end of the lesson, he asked us all to move to one end of the lawn. We were to run toward the other end at a signal and fall on the ground, facedown, when we heard his whistle.

We did as we were told. The drill lasted for about a half hour in the hot sun. At the end of the exercise, our uniforms were in ruins. Our lunch, saved for us by the cooks, was cold. But mostly we were tired from let-down expectations induced by the drill. We had looked forward to something much more demanding and exciting. Some of the older girls grumbled.

"Who ever heard of trying to save your life from something that is flying way up in the sky by falling on the ground? These army people are mad, just plain mad. How could a moving airplane kill people on the ground anyway?"

It took the nuns and the teachers the rest of the day and all night to get the students back to normal routines. Study Hall was a disaster because nobody had any sleep during siesta and supper stretched everyone's nerves. Students ignored the study hall prefect's threats about punishments we had never heard of. Instead, we gathered around in little groups outside the building, discussing the impending crisis. Later that evening there were rumors about Reverend Mother Principal's secret meeting with the prefects. It was said that Reverend Mother Principal, who knew something about wars, was very upset and worried. She told the prefects to be vigilant. They should report any strange visitors to her. News of guerilla fighters spread like wildfire. Stories of school closures in other parts of the country suddenly became meaningful. Reverend Mother Principal said that the nuns would have to leave if the war reached our part of the country.

In the dormitories, students broke down in tears as it became more and more obvious that the threat of war was real. What would happen to us? Would we have to join the army? Our dormitory prefect, Idorenyin Okon, told us to get ready for marriage, war rations, and death. She told us horror stories of the Hundred Years' War and the War of Roses which Velvet and I were sure she had made up but which struck fear in our hearts nonetheless. She said that by the time the war ended we would all be dead and forgotten and that we had better perfect our Latin skills because that was the language the angels spoke at the gates of Heaven. Since I was not very good at languages, I knew I was doomed. My expertise in Latin began and ended with "Salve Magister," and I knew that our Latin teacher did not have much hope for me, even with that one phrase. I prepared for a long sojourn in Hell. As I drifted off to sleep, I vowed I would go to confession . . .

For the next few nights, the nuns slept very little as they patrolled the dormitories, counseling or admonishing students who woke up from nightmares about war, death, and various versions of decimated futures. The radio became very important in our lives as we began to pay more attention to regional and national news. Fear came to Our Lady of Peace Secondary School for Girls and took permanent residence in the dormitories, classrooms, and refectories. Every other day, parents from distant parts of the country came to take their children home. Those of us from immediate and surrounding regions took on new responsibilities as hostesses to our colleagues who had suddenly become our guests. Reverend Mother Principal no longer traveled far without a male teacher from the area and two or three prefects.

Grace, Velvet, and I finally understood that the war was real when the first teacher from a different part of Obodo left for her hometown. She was our French teacher and a very active faculty member. Every student's friend, she provided much-needed intervention between the students and the foreign administrators. She was young and full of life, and most of the students believed nothing until Miss Sola Ogun confirmed it. To us she also made the most sense because she was well educated and single. This, to us, meant that she had not completely joined the world of grown-ups and had a better understanding

of youth and its yearnings. Many times she invited us to sump-
tuous meals at her house, allowing us to play her records and
borrow her books. Her departure left us empty but with a certain understanding of the reality of the emergency that we had
been unable to grasp so far.

After Miss Ogun left, most of the students packed their
things, ready to leave at a moment's notice. Gone was our joy
of striving for an endless horizon of futures. Within these
past few weeks, our childhood had died, our youth had gone. In
their places was a strange and uncertain adulthood waiting for
an even more precarious future. We began to get ready for the
war. We waited.

One evening my aunt's eldest son came to visit me at school.
It was in the middle of the week, so I thought someone had
died. It was worse. My father had become an officer in the
Emergency Army. Now I lived in fear of the news of my father's death.

Outside, in the nearby village of Ikot Nyin and in the township of Isong Idung, life went on as usual. The senior girls
who went into the town or the prefects who accompanied Reverend Mother Principal on her travels said that nothing much
had changed in people's lives in the area. Every day on the
radio there was news of deaths in new war fronts; of people
abandoning or being forced out of their homes in different
parts of the country; of the rising State of Emergency. Most of
us began to wish that our parents would come and take us
away from the nightmare that was slowly enveloping us. Many
nights I cried myself to sleep wondering if ours would be next
on the long list of closed schools.

Velvet, my neighbor in the dorm, lost interest in school. She
no longer talked nonstop. She became morose and introspec-
tive. I found myself wishing that she would become her talka-
tive self again. I wished we could all go back four or five weeks
or even to that fateful day when the officer came and disrupted

our lives with his speech about taking cover and the State of Emergency.

One night, I tried to talk to Velvet after lights-out, the way we used to before the Emergency. But she only answered in monosyllables. Finally, she told me to stop bothering her and then she started to cry. Idorenyin, our dormitory prefect, turned on a flashlight and we all gathered around Velvet. After many minutes of questions, during which some of the other girls also started to cry, Velvet revealed that her brother, who was a student at St. Michael's Secondary School for Boys, visited her earlier in the week and told her that her soldier uncle was dead. Apparently he died during a skirmish at a railway station while on guard duty. They were not quite sure what happened, but Velvet's brother said some demonstrators opposed to the Emergency had attacked their uncle and three others. Later that night, when the Reverend Mother on duty came into our dorm, she found most of us sleeping fitfully, two or three girls per bed. Idorenyin said that the Reverend Mother spent most of the night in the common room of our dorm, waiting, her fingers moving swiftly from bead to bead on her rosary.

One morning, on our way back from Mass, the emergency bell began to ring. According to the general instructions each student received on admission to Our Lady of Peace, that meant we should proceed to Assembly Hall immediately. As the big, long room filled with students and faculty, I couldn't help but marvel at the change that had taken place in the school in such a short time. Our numbers had diminished significantly. Unlike the day of the air raid speech a few weeks before, students spoke in subdued whispers.

"What's wrong?"

"Is the war here?"

"Is it a good idea for all of us to be in one place?"

Speculations grew and spread as we waited for what we knew

could only be more bad news. Reverend Mother Principal got up on the stage. Everyone stopped talking.

Assembly Hall was not a regular meeting place for faculty and students. It was used for assembly only twice a term: at the beginning and at the end. In between, it was usually a jolly place. This was where we held Sunday Dance every other Sunday evening after supper, dancing to highlife, juju music, waltz, the jig, and the cha-cha-cha. Here, we shared the latest dance steps and held dance competitions. Here was where we entertained school guests after interschool debates and other significant events.

In this hall many students met their first boyfriends, sometimes their future husbands. This was the only place on the entire campus where a student could be caught in a boy's embrace and get away with it. Assembly Hall was open, warm, and receptive. From its walls, pictures of nuns who had taught here, along with the picture of the wealthy founding nun with the intense brown eyes, overlooked our entrances and departures from Our Lady's. On Dance Sundays we ignored her eminent presence, dancing to local and foreign music, executing moves that only teenagers' bodies can attempt. Even Mother Principal was known to have attempted some new dance steps or smiled and moved on at the sight of a student shyly embracing a boyfriend on the wide verandas of Assembly Hall.

To all the students of Our Lady of Peace, Assembly Hall was memorable because of its capacity to accommodate all our dreams as we learned, recited, and performed our favorite poems, dances, songs, and science projects. Individually and in groups, we presented here to our teachers, our parents, and to each other. This was where, twice a term, the Drama Club showed off without risk or ridicule the variety of talents its members could boast. For the junior classes, the stage in Assembly Hall was the music room where everyone got their first piano lesson and Reverend Mother Music played to each class songs from *The Sound of Music* and *The Wizard of Oz* and taught us about music from other lands. Here, she allowed us to be young and silly as we laughed at our efforts to learn and master the incongruous, nonrhythmic music from places we had only read about, in history and geography books. Assembly Hall was not a place to announce bad news. Even before Reverend Mother Principal got on the stage, some of the students were sobbing quietly.

Perhaps it had to do with the violation of Assembly Hall expectations that was about to take place. Perhaps the older students could not stand the thought of seeing that happen. Maybe it was the fact that there had been no real public acknowledgment of our collective and individual fears until now. True, the Reverend Mothers had tried their best to prepare us for the worst. But they had never till now tried to tell us, collectively, what that worst could be, and we did not want to know. Not now. And definitely not in Assembly Hall, which harbored some of the foundations of our dreams for the future. Reverend Mother Principal adjusted her wimple and waited for silence. She told us amid sniffles and sobs from students. She told us what we had been waiting for but dreading to hear for weeks. She told us that Our Lady of Peace School for Girls was on the list of schools to be closed that week. The war fronts were becoming more and more unpredictable and it was no longer safe to keep the school open. We were to go back to the dormitories and pack our things and come back to Assembly Hall after lunch for a fitting farewell because some of us would never see each other again.

There would be no classes. The nuns would start making the arrangements for the vehicles that would take us to our various destinations. No one was to try to leave the school premises on her own because the nuns wanted to be able to give an account of every single student in the school if necessary. There would be sign-up sheets for the various destinations and they would try to accommodate every student's needs. At the end of Mother Principal's announcement, Assembly Hall broke down in uncontrollable sobbing. Nobody waited for the usual protocols for dismissal as students left to share or hide their grief on the veranda or the lawn.

I stood outside on the veranda for a while, waiting for I know not what, when I noticed that Grace was standing beside me. As usual, she looked as neat as a pin but her eyes were red.

"Nwanyieze, do you need help packing?" Grace asked, smiling through her grief.

"Me? My things have been packed since Miss Ogun left," I said.

"Mine too. What do you want to do?"

"Let's go and eat first. Since we don't know what's next, it's always wise to have a full stomach. That way, if anything happens, we'll at least be full."

"What's on the menu today? Do you know?"

"No. Probably bread and egg. That's all we've been eating for days."

"They're saying that the market is not good these days. It's getting more and more difficult to move from one part of the country to another."

"In that case, let's go and eat. There may not be anything for lunch," I tried to joke.

The refectory was on the other side of the campus. Since we had nothing to do till lunch, we took our time. Besides, since many of the students were going toward the dorms, there was no crowd to beat.

We walked slowly, exchanging news of family members and our expectations of the Emergency. We both had male cousins who had joined the Emergency Army and we wondered what they would look like in uniform. The sky was clear and the flowers bloomed their brilliant colors. There was a slight breeze. I raised my face to it, wanting its coolness to relax my tense face and cool my eyes. As we approached the path to the refectory, we heard the sound of an airplane in the distance. Velvet, who was standing on the veranda of the refectory, started calling to us to run inside the building.

"Nwanyieze, Grace! Nwanyieze! Grace! Run! Can't you hear the plane?" Velvet was jumping up and down, waving and urging us to hurry up and get into the building. I could see that she was laughing. We started to run toward her. Soon, we were also laughing hard as we ran toward the building.

"Nwanyieze! Come inside! Gr-a-a-a-ce!"

Students were streaming out of the building, looking up into the blue sky.

"Where is it?"

"Where's the airplane?"

"Have you seen it?"

Girls filled the lawn in front of the building. I turned around, looking back toward Assembly Hall, which we had just left. There were students all over the schoolgrounds. Some people were already lying facedown on the green lawn, just like the officer had taught us.

Soon, the plane came into full view. It was flying so low it looked like it was riding on the rooftops of our school buildings. Its engine roared like unending thunder, shaking the ground under our feet. But it flew past the school. Its fearful sound merged into a distant silence that left us wishing for yesterday, or else tomorrow.

Some of the students started joking about how afraid they had been of the encounter. Grace and I stood on the lawn in front of the refectory. Uncertain what to do, we stood and waited, laughing at our unfounded fears. Finally, Velvet decided to go inside the building to get some food. She told us to keep watch while she went to get us our share of the bread and eggs.

"It's coming back! It's coming back!"

Again people flung themselves on the lawns. I felt Grace

pull me to the ground. There was a blinding flash and a noise so loud I can still hear it today. As I fell, my mind flew in a thousand different directions as the earth beneath split into countless pieces. As I fell, I heard my grandmother and my aunt telling me over many years of schooling to be careful.

"Don't learn more than we need," they cautioned.

As I fell, I saw myself smiling at their lack of understanding. I heard myself telling them that we were only joining the rest of the world as it progressed to better things. I remembered the many times they had waited with me for the taxi or mammy wagon that took me away to the township where my parents work, or to school. I heard again the tearful good-byes. I wondered who would tell them what had happened to our school, to our dreams. I felt my body hit the ground. I tasted cold, raw earth and green grass. Something big flew over my head and fell a few yards from where I lay.

It was a piece of roof from the refectory. Then the screaming started. It was as if the screaming would never stop. It still hasn't. Finally, the earth pulled itself together and I opened my eyes. There was smoke coming from where both the refectory and Assembly Hall used to be.

By the time the ambulance came from Isong Idung, Reverend Mother Music, Velvet, and Reverend Mother H. were dead. The Reverend Mothers who died had not left the Hall after the emergency assembly. Mother Principal had asked them to prepare the hall for one last performance before the students' departure.

Reverend Mother Principal was inconsolable. Several other people, including two of the cooks, were dead. Many were wounded.

All day long, the radio announced the incident. Parents came to pick up their daughters. Those whose children were wounded were sent to the general hospital in town. Later, a requiem mass was said for the souls of those who had been killed in the school's bombing. That night, most of us refused to go back to the dormitories. When we found out that the Reverend Mothers would not even let us sleep on the floor in their convent, we slept on the chapel floor. We were hurt and angry at their rejection and could not pray. I hoped God would forgive us for sleeping on the chapel floor. The next day, students waited on the main driveway for the taxis, private cars, mammy wagons, and buses.

Grace left in a taxi early in the afternoon. All the girls from my dorm were gone. The nuns stood in the shade of a veranda. My father had sent an army jeep and a driver for me. The driver, dressed in an army uniform, greeted me and loaded my things into the back of the jeep. I stood by and watched until he finished and then he helped me into the passenger seat. As he drove off, I looked back and started to wave at the few remaining groups of students waiting for transportation to their different homes. But somehow I couldn't wave. I realized that I couldn't recognize anyone among the sad, unfriendly faces of my schoolmates. It was not that I didn't know their names. I did. But, I did not know them. None of them smiled or waved at me as the jeep took me through the school gates.

The Last Push

Two shots rang out in the still, hot Sunday afternoon. The mother hen outside stopped in her tracks, quiet in her anticipation of death.

"Oh my God!" said Chika and Nwaku simultaneously. The small enamel basin clattered to the floor, scattering enamel chips and the pumpkin leaves Chika was cleaning for the evening meal all over the cement floor.

"Air raid!" someone shouted outside.

"Shut up!" several voices said together from nearby houses.

"Suffering Christ!" Chika could not remember when she started hearing the note of hysteria in her neighbors' voices. At first, Akasi people enjoyed the antics of the fighters and bombers, cheering the pilots on as they maneuvered the winged messengers of death. Always applauding skill and competence, they marveled as the planes cut through clear, hot blue sky, dipping, swooping, and dropping death from heaven.

That was before the enemy pilots knew this area of Biafra well. Back then they dropped most of their bombs in nearby bushes and uninhabited forests. But they had acquired the precision that follows practice. And no wonder. Two and a half years of dropping bombs in an area as small as Biafra had become enough. As their aim became more accurate, the nerves of the people on the ground stretched to the breaking point. Everyone hoped for the end of this war which, without warning, had become a part of their lives. These days even five-year-olds could tell the difference between the deadly screeches of the latest explosives from the shrills of older, more familiar ones. These win-the-war children could tell different kinds of artillery from armored cars and tankers.

Two days before, Chika overheard a conversation between a three- and a five-year-old.

"Why aren't people going to the farms today?" asked the three-year-old.

"Oh, don't you know that somebody died?" replied the older boy.

"Hmmm? But there was no 'Take cover!' yesterday," said the younger child, who had reached the conclusion that only planes kill people. A loud explosion brought Chika back to the present.

"What did it hit?"

"Chineke! It hit something!"

"I see smoke. It hit something."

"Stay where you are. Don't move!" voices warned as the sky vibrated with the roaring of death-bearing craft.

Men, women, and children ran in small, silent groups toward the road to the stream. Before the air raid started, Chika didn't know that most of her neighbors were home instead of in the surrounding farm areas, bushes, and forests, taking cover.

Everyone had hurried home from the early and speedy church service. People worried about clear-blue-sky days because the planes rarely came when it rained. Most people prayed for rainy Sundays so they could rest from the treks into the farmlands to take cover. Today, it had seemed Akasi was blessed with the unheard-of gift of a blue-sky Sunday unmarked with air raids. Until now, there had been no sounds of distant firing from the nearest war fronts, no soothing buzz of a peaceful passenger plane in a war-torn zone, no sounds of children playing familiar childhood games, no echoes from wooden pestles pounding delicacies for Sunday dinners.

"They hit the Apostolic church! Many people are dead!" A young man spread the news as he dashed for better cover.

Two weeks without air raids and Chika had almost fallen into the false rhythm of a peaceful world. Now her anger was tinged with fear and helplessness as the make-believe world she had snatched for herself shattered.

From the day of the first air raid she had lived in constant fear. The days were filled with spine-tingling dread of skies torn apart by frenzied aircraft loaded with death. Each morning she woke up poised to take cover, protecting a flavorless wartime life. Every night was a take-cover nightmare from which she woke in sweating fear of winged death from heaven. Every day she wished death would go back to being normal.

"Mama," whispered her daughter urgently, "what should we do? Where should we go? Everyone is running into the forests. Mama, let's take cover!"

"No!" she answered. "We are staying in this house today. I'm too tired to run." She pulled the girl close, wanting to protect them both.

But the two rooms she shared with her children offered no protection. Uche, her husband, was gone. Three weeks after he announced a yearning to join the Emergency Army, he became a soldier and left. In the year since he left, she had steeled herself for any kind of news about him.

"Mama, I'm going to take cover outside," Nwaku said. Chika grabbed her as she reached the door. Nwaku struggled free, causing both of them to fall by the doorpost. The child got up first. Slowly, she put one foot outside.

"Come back inside, you fool!" Chika shouted. "Do you want to kill yourself?"

"Shut up!"

"Shhhhh!"

"Do you want to kill us?" Hushed voices came from their neighbors.

"Where's Grandfather and everybody?"

"They went to take cover. Stop talking."

Chika fumed at her own stubbornness. If she had run for the protective cover of the forests earlier, she would not be here waiting to be killed by people to whom she owed nothing. The harsh, furious noises of the killer craft formed the Sunday afternoon sky into a ceiling of pandemonium. Yet a child's whimper or a dropped cup next door sounded loud enough that she felt the enemy pilot would hear them. Another wave of people moved quietly into the bushes and bunkers around the compound. The hen that had been scratching for food with its chickens now sat on the veranda, the chickens under its wings, quiet. Suddenly, a herd of goats and sheep came out of nowhere. Simultaneously, one of the jet fighters swooped. There was a blinding flash. Screams and pleas for life mixed with the receding thunder of the fighter jets. Chika tripped on a chair and fell again as she reached for her daughter. This time, neither woman nor child moved as the noise outside reached that peak where sound and silence merge and the living can hear eternity. The deathlike quiet that followed cut the Sunday afternoon like a knife. She heard the day die at the same time the people came to a motionless life. Chika picked herself up. She wiped the sweat from her forehead with the end of her *lappa* and pulled Nwaku from behind a chair.

"Are you alright?"

"Hmmm."

"Get up."

The child stood up slowly. Chika felt her all over. No scratches, no blood.

"You're alright. Open your eyes. Sit down." Her voice was barely harsh enough to hide a quaver. Her hands shook as she began to dry the child's tears. More antiaircraft shots rang out as the planes came back.

"There're three! My God! They want to finish us today,"

said Chika, pointing at bullet holes in the red-brown earth outside. "We can't go outside now. They'll see us. Look, that hen is dead. They saw those goats moving and fired at our compound." Her eyes swept the room.

For the hundredth time, she surveyed the front room. She realized there was nowhere to hide. This room, which had been her refuge for the past year, suddenly merged with the war zones out there, even as she felt its walls move closer, trapping her. She pulled Nwaku to her, shielding the little body with hers.

"Ma, what will we do?"

"Stop crying. Stop crying, my child. They will soon leave. It will soon be over."

Mother and child dared not look outside again. From the sound of things, those pilots and their crew were enjoying themselves firing at and bombing the ungodly rebels. Chika opened a suitcase and dug into it, scattering clothes all over the bed and floor. She found a dark-green wrapper and a black blouse and began to exchange them for the ones she was wearing.

"Where are you going, Ma?"

"To look for your sister."

"Can I . . ."

"Wait!" They spoke together as another explosion shook the house to its foundations. The family picture crashed to the floor, shattering glass. For the next ten minutes it was impossible to distinguish between enemy and return fire from the many antiaircraft posts all over the town.

"That was close." Nwaku held on to Chika as another explosion resounded nearby.

"Hmmm . . . ," replied Chika as she continued to change her clothes.

"Ma, don't leave me here by myself. I'll be dead by the time you come back." Chika did not know how to soothe her.

"Ma, I'm going with you."

"No, I can't take you. We'll both get killed." She held the child close. "I'll be back soon. I promise."

"Oh, you are home." The woman and the child both started. They were relieved to see the tall, slim youth who had tiptoed into the room. It was Uchenna, her only son. He spoke in a low voice, for, in spite of the noise above them, the town was quiet.

"You should start packing at once. Enemy troops have come in under cover of the air raid. Where's Udo?"

"Who? Oh, she went to fetch water for my mother."

"The Federal troops. Enemy troops. The radio says that the UN gave them troops to make one final attack on Biafra. This thing you're seeing," he indicated the sky to include the jet fighters and the noise, "is not going to stop until Biafra is finished or has surrendered. One of the lieutenants from the army camp is going around telling people to leave Akasi. He saw us taking cover under the big *achi* tree at the village square." Uchenna was throwing shirts and dresses in a medium-size suitcase which he took from under one of the beds. Chika started to repack the suitcase she had rifled through earlier. Her mind was in turmoil.

The UN peacekeeping forces. She had heard about them on the radio. The first time was early in the war when the radio said that France and Gabon had recognized Biafra. Recognized. As if the people needed to be recognized in order to exist. But you never knew with all this government and country business. If you came from a place like Akasi, you knew you were there no matter who or what did not recognize you. But with this government business, you had to go to France to recognize yourself. After Gabon recognized the new Biafra, everybody and their mother danced the recognition dance. It was a war dance of recognition that Chika and her friends danced that day, thinking it meant the end of the war. But like most things brought by the war, it turned out to be the beginning of months of fear, uncertainty, hunger, and, always, death. She had put all her energy and hope into that dance of recognition of strife, the real announcement of the beginning of months of violence, sudden death, the conscription of youths into the emergency forces, the closing of schools, terror, and insecurity. War.

There followed many more promises of recognition, soldiers, weapons, peace, food; promises of a return to normalcy and a familiar world. Chika used to ask Uche how they could make peace by killing people. But Uche believed in gova'ment.

"Gova'ment knows the world differently from real people," he said. "Gova'ment knows that the more enemy troops we kill, the better our chances of having peace in this country." So he joined the Emergency Army.

"Are you saying that these people have sent soldiers of peace from abroad to kill our people so we can have peace?" Uchenna nodded. Chika sucked in her breath.

"Maybe this time they'll succeed," she fumed. "One thing is certain, I will not dance through the nineteen villages of Akasi again just because of any peace soldiers with promises of war. I'll get out of this thing alive. I'll survive their peaceful bullets and their peace soldiers." She snapped the suitcase shut.

"Go and bring two pots and some enamel plates from the kitchen," she said to Uchenna. He looked at her in disbelief. The kitchen was in the back of the house. But she held his gaze.

"Go! We have to hurry." He dropped his eyes and started for the back of the house, stopping long enough to avoid another spattering of bullets as a swooping fighter sprayed the compound.

"Are you there?" asked Chika in a low but carrying voice.

"Hmmm."

"Don't move. Wait for them to move out a little, then come back, you hear?"

"Yes."

She did not know when she started praying under her breath. Her anger, mixed with her helpless prayer, fueled her hot and rising blood. She hoped Udo was safe.

"Please, don't take my child. Please don't take her too!" she implored the raging noise outside. This would be their third evacuation in eighteen months and Chika knew the sequence: pack in a hurry, move under intense firing, settle for a few months; pack, move . . . A year ago, they had returned to their hometown, Akasi, because it seemed farthest from any of the war fronts. In that time, Akasi had become completely surrounded. It would be difficult to escape alive this time. There was nowhere else to run.

"Are you ready?" One of their neighbors, Mrs. Uwadiegwu, was leaving with her daughter, Stella. Her husband and their son, Uba, had joined the emergency forces soon after the family moved here. Stella and Udo were friends. Hardworking and friendly, Mama Stella bore her wartime experiences with dignity. Light household items were strapped to the handles and sides of the suitcases on their heads.

"I think they're gone," she said, sweeping the skies with one hand.

"That's good. Be careful. They've probably only gone to refuel and reload. They'll be back soon. Go carefully."

"Please, hurry up!" Stella said. "Tell Udo we're going to be in the usual take-cover place at the wine tapper's shed."

"We'll be there soon."

Uchenna returned from the kitchen and in a short time they were ready to leave.

"Did you pack some clothes for your father?"

"Yes," Uchenna answered gruffly. He was still angry at having to go to the kitchen. His father would never have done that, he thought. He never let Uche and his sisters carry heavy loads on their heads either. He would have hired a taxi. Everyone called his father the young millionaire. Uchenna missed him. He missed his father's laughter and reassuring smile during these fear-filled days. But the enemy troops were here and no one would be driving a car for the next few weeks because the roads were always the first targets.

Uchenna waited for his mother to finish packing. If he left without them, it could be months before he saw them again. There were countless stories of children separated from their families during evacuations.

Chika pulled out another suitcase, quickly inspected its contents, then locked it and left it on the bed.

"Let's go."

"Why the second suitcase?" Uchenna asked.

"It's for Udo, in case she comes home before going into the forest. Let's go."

"Listen!" Uchenna said as they stepped away from the door.

Fighter jets could be heard rumbling toward them. Within moments confusion reigned again in the sky. Chika and her children crouched in the room. Nwaku was whimpering, her hands over her ears. Chika didn't bother to count the planes this time. Another fifteen minutes and all was quiet again.

"Let's go." Chika felt as if she had been saying that all day.

They made it to the village square without mishap. Three old men were sitting under the achi tree talking to an army officer.

"You've come out?" It was both a greeting and a question about the eventful day.

"Yes," Chika replied.

"Aren't you going to take cover?" Nwaku asked them.

"No, my child," said one of the men. "We will be here to greet them when they arrive. They should know that people live here."

"But they will kill you!" Nwaku was concerned.

"They have no use for old people like us. No, they will not kill us. The ancestors forbid it." He spat ritually. She looked at her mother anxiously. Chika's smile was reassuring.

"I will be here with them," the uniformed officer said to Nwaku. He was from a nearby village. "Go toward the farms and forests. The enemy troops go down the tarmac first to clear it of moving objects."

Chika steered her charges toward the road to Oboroji stream. At the corner, she looked back at the achi tree. Would it still be there when they returned? Would they return to its safety and shade during this lifetime? Chika's heart filled with dread.

The achi tree stood like a sentinel at the center of the village. Rain or shine, its leaves provided shelter from the sky. Its huge roots jutted out, extending fifty or more feet from the huge trunk. A white piece of ritual cloth tied around the trunk protected the tree from the curious and the profane. In places its roots formed large receptacles for water, which had collected over generations. People came from surrounding villages seeking permission from the village elders to use this water for sacrifices or to cure nameless illnesses. Some of the jutting roots facing the playground were as smooth as kitchen stools from years of use by young and old. In the evenings the women turned the tree's shelter into *ogwumabiri*, the evening market where they sold fresh vegetables and smoke-dried fish and other condiments for evening meals.

Throughout the year, different dance groups from Akasi and the neighboring towns performed here. A popular meeting place, it was seldom empty. "Meet me at the achi tree," children reminded each other as they prepared to go to the stream, to fetch firewood, or to play. "Your child is at the achi tree," parents cautioned each other, worrying that children would come to nothing if allowed to spend too much time there. Yet the achi tree at the village square remained the marker for stability, social freedom, and unity. As the war progressed, it became the safest place in Akasi. No bullet had penetrated its thick leaves to the village square below. It became the source for war news as people, cars, mammy wagons, and regular and army trucks stopped at the permanent market that sprang up under the tree. During air raids, people did not run from the safety of the achi tree into the surrounding open spaces.

Before the war, Akasi people swore by its presence to validate themselves, their words, and their actions. But the opening of the achi tree to win-the-war activities made them cautious about news heard under its shade. These days if someone called you "Radio *ukwu-achi*," as opposed to "Radio Biafra," it meant you were an unconvincing messenger. Throughout the war, the achi tree did not lose its power as one of the stabilizers of the community. Instead, Oboroji village learned to adjust to the vicissitudes of war and transition. This meant that strangers could not be expected to know that it was risky to tell untruths under the tree's watchful, cool shade. Chika sent a silent message to the spirit of the tree and turned toward the stream. She knew she would return. As the little group reached the bottom of the first hill, they saw a woman kneeling near the bushes just before the log bridge across the stream. Nwaku, who was walking behind Uchenna, stopped to let her mother pass.

"Chi-n-eke-e-e-e!" Chika's scream resounded in the valley. It was Mama Stella.

"Ma, they'll hear you!" said Nwaku. "Ma, please stop! You'll make the planes come back."

"What shall I do?" Chika wailed. The dead woman's head-load had rolled into the stream.

"Mama!" was all the boy could whisper. Chika knelt beside the body. The children stood back, not sure if the woman would rise or not. The bullet had gone into the left side of her head and had not come out the other side. Congealed blood hung from her open mouth.

Chika cried. She had not known the woman well. But she knew that Mama Stella's main hope was to go back to her own people after the war. After the war. That phrase which had become both a hope and a destination these past three years. Biafrans spoke of after the war with the certainty that Christians speak of Heaven. No one knew if all were worthy of after-the-war grace but it was a promise held for those who believed in an eternal goodness reserved by the Universe for nations under stress.

Chika cried for Mama Stella, for herself, and for a nation gone berserk in its search for Peace and Unity. She cried for a nation whose madness allowed it to purchase and borrow weapons from unknown lands to kill its own people for reasons forgotten. She cried for Mama Stella, who did not have to go to a war front to die, for her own inability to protect her children from the incessant assaults of the war. Her tears fell on the back of the dead woman, wetting her blouse. The patch of wetness brought Chika back to her senses.

She stood up and scanned the area. Stella had fallen facedown, her hands outstretched toward the trunk of a tree, as if in supplication.

"Why not?" Chika said. "Why not? Trees are the only things that have remained still all these years. Only the trees in Biafra are blessed."

"Mama," called Uchenna in a low, frightened voice.

"Mama. Please don't cry anymore. Mama, please, let's go!" the children pleaded.

In the distance the clear blue Sunday sky rumbled again. Chika braced herself for another air raid.

Throughout the raids that Sunday, people trickled into the valley and forests. It was three days before Udo and her grandmother found Chika and the rest. The first raid caught Udo at the stream, where she said the planes flew so low she could see the pilots' faces. Every night she woke up screaming for Chika. After a few nights of trying to find her among the sleeping bodies of other people's children, Chika took Udo and Nwaku to sleep with her in the women's section.

Her mother worried about Chika's brothers and sisters and their families. It was difficult to have conversation because people were not allowed to speak above a whisper in the forest. The only bold noises came from the fighter planes going to proclaim peace to neighboring towns. Each day, the older people declared continuing silence and emphasized the importance of smokeless cooking fires.

The week before, some tired-looking soldiers had come into the valley from a back road and ambushed one of the camps, but they were overpowered and killed. After that, waiting for peace was even harder as movement became more restricted. People whispered survival stories all day.

"Nne, have you eaten?"

"Is it that mess Udo cooks? What am I going to eat that for? When you were her age, I thought the best thing was to send you to that mission school. You don't know one wild leaf from another because I sent you away to the mission to learn books. That is why I came to find you and the children. If I had known, I would at least have taught you about the land and our people before sending you away to strangers." Nne was a feisty woman used to making her own way. This was not the first time she had voiced her regret about sending Chika to the mission school.

When the war closed the schools, Chika, an elementary school teacher, learned farm work. She joined in the daily treks into the farmlands, adjusting to the ceaseless fight with weeds in the cassava and yam plots and the hopelessness of the war efforts.

"I've learned many things about farming, Nne. It's not very hard."

"I know. But that's not what you wanted to do. This," she said, indicating the camp, "is not who you wanted to be."

"This is not who anybody wants to be. But that doesn't mean we should stop eating. The war will soon be over and we'll go back home."

"Which home? The one you and Uche lost in the big town?"

"We will build another one. You will see. He will go back to his trade and we will build again." She was trying to convince herself. Before the crises, they had a good life in Elu-ugwu, where he owned several big stalls in the market. They had a big house and rented out some rooms. When the town fell, they lost everything. Uche started a small trade in another town but they had to move again. Finally, they returned to Oboroji, to Uche's parents' house.

Udo brought some food. The children laughed as Nne made faces at the saltless food.

"Don't worry," Udo consoled her, "Uchenna has gone fishing. If he kills anything, even frogs, we will have a tasty meal today."

"Any day I eat frogs, count me out of the living," Nne vowed.

"Don't say that," Udo counseled. "In our school books, it says that frogs are delicacies for the French people."

"Then go and cook for *them*." She tried a little more of the tasteless food. "Is that really what your book says? Frogs?" Chika and Udo nodded. One of the men motioned to them to speak in whispers.

"Were you really that close to a real bomb that Sunday?" Udo asked for the thousandth time. Chika nodded. Though she would never understand these win-the-war children and their hunger for war stories, she whispered the story again.

That last Sunday, Chika had just enough time to shove Uchenna and Nwaku into the bushes as a bomb exploded over the stream. Uchenna's scream could be heard for miles around. Nwaku fainted. Later, people said it must have been a stray bomb. When Nwaku came to, she was screaming, "Ma, please touch my hand. Please, Ma, hold me! Ma, am I dead? Where are we?"

Chika assured her many times that she was not dead. Soon, people came down the hill. Those from Ezi-Ukwu compound started wailing for the dead woman and her child. Mother and child were quickly buried in shallow graves close to the road. Afterward, Chika and her children joined the trek into the forest. For the rest of that day they could hear the jet fighters evacuating the town. Those who stayed till the end brought news of the peace soldiers leading the enemy troops through the town.

Some people refused to leave the town, preferring to welcome the newcomers and show them around. Chika and her friends called them saboteurs. What was there to show after years of suffering and strife? Were they going to show them those who had died from air raids, kwashiorkor, and frustration? Would they show them the hurried weddings, spiritless New Yam Festivals, speedy church services, indifferent breakfasts, and saltless suppers? What would they show to gun-carrying peace soldiers?

Her first question to the bringers of peace would be about her husband. Where was he? No, not the man who would come back from the war, but the man she married. The one she lost during the first year of the war: the enterprising, smiling, dauntless man known to his friends, neighbors, and customers as the young millionaire.

She would have to live with a war-ravaged stranger, pretending she cared for and understood the new person they had trained to kill. Or she would take the children back to her mother's house.

"Not to my house. May the ancestors forbid a bad thing!" Nne spit ritually. "Both of us would be dead, just like that." Nne snapped her fingers. "No, you will not leave him. What has he done to you? He went to protect us. Is that bad?"

"But I never wanted to marry a soldier. How can a woman who never wanted to marry a soldier live with an ex-soldier? Why should I live with a man trained to kill others for the sake of peace?"

"You will not leave him. I will have no hand in it." Nne was emphatic.

Later that evening, Chika repacked their things in the suitcases. No one said anything. These were hard times and the rules of life as they knew it had changed.

When the sun rose, Chika was gone. She did not take the children or the suitcases. All day the people in the camp shifted, restless for Chika and her gentle smile. But nobody openly asked her whereabouts. If anyone could be relied on in Oboroji village, it was Chika. As constant as the day was long, turning saboteur was not within her ability. But her absence meant only one thing: she had gone to the peace soldiers. She was a harlot. By early afternoon, mothers began to call their children away from Nwaku. Udo's friends did not invite her to bathe in the stream. Nne was worried. Sending Chika to school had been her idea. Her husband had warned her that book learning would ruin their family.

When the sun passed the middle of the sky and there was no news of Chika, Udo was afraid. First her father, now her mother, was gone. Two years before, she had been the envy of her friends. She had an adoring father and a loving mother. Over a year ago, he left to become a soldier. Today her mother left without a word. Udo discussed all these things with Uchenna after their lunch of tasteless yam pottage and fresh fish.

"I am going to look around," Uchenna said. Udo raised tear-filled eyes to her brother. Was he going to leave too? Neither child said Chika's name for fear of what they thought they knew. Better that someone went looking. Then, if she was dead, they would all know. Uchenna left. His friend Egbe, who always played soccer with him, was waiting at the other end of the camp.

Nwaku's demands for an evening meal were just beginning to irritate her sister and grandmother when they heard a joyful scream. Uchenna and Egbe stood at the edge of the camp. Their grins filled the forest floor, illuminating the camp. Behind them was Chika, a white enamel basin on her head. Her smile turned into loud laughter as she approached them.

"You should see your faces. Did you think I was dead or what? Someone please help me put this load down." When none of the women moved to help her, Udo and the two boys ran quickly to her.

"What's the matter?" she asked loudly.

"They think you're a saboteur. Oh, Chineke! Mama, are you a saboteur?" Udo sobbed loudly, ignoring the rules about silence.

"Saboteur? What do you mean? Saboteur? Do I look like a betrayer of my people to any of you? What kind of saboteur would I make? Let me tell you something, the war is over. The news is everywhere. On the radio. Everywhere. The war ended the day after that air raid Sunday. Some say it ended before that. We didn't know it here because no one brought a radio."

"What are you talking about?" someone interrupted.

"What about all the gunshots?" asked another.

"I am telling you, it's finished. Look, if you doubt me, here are some onions and salt!" She held up a large onion and brought out some cooking salt wrapped in newspaper, letting some trickle to the ground.

"Stop that!" one of the women shrieked. "Don't waste cooking salt like that!"

"Don't worry," Chika said, "there's more salt where that came from." Her self-assurance brought the women over. She began to unload the enamel basin. "Udo, make a fire! Here's some dried fish and *garri*. Make some soup. Nne, here's some aspirin for your headache. Who needs some salt? Udo, give people salt so they can cook." The forest stirred in renewed hope. Questions filled the camp. "What happened?" "Where did you get all this?"

Chika settled down on a log and told a story of peace in the form of shops once more filled with basic products at reasonable prices. Creeping up the last hill into the village, she had promised herself that she would kill the first peace soldier who dared to look at her. She saw no one until she reached the achi tree. Two of the oldest men of Oboroji village greeted her. She told them that many people were alive and hiding in the forests. The old men told her that the war was over and that she should go and bring people back to the village.

While the old men were telling Chika their story, a peace soldier came up and greeted Chika. He looked nice and clean and healthy. Yes, he had a gun. They shot only goats and chickens with the guns. The soldiers were all over Akasi. They had already killed two men who did not want them living in their houses. Their camp was at the elementary school on the hill.

That night everyone in the camp ate salted food and told win-the-war stories till late. As she lay between her two daughters on her pile of leaves, Chika shivered as she remembered the soldier who had given her the money for the food. She now knew what an ex-soldier husband would feel like.

Chika scooped dried red pepper from a sack onto the display table in her stall.

"Customer, buy here! This is good pepper. Look! Customer!" She had yet to acquire the aggressive but pleasant voice of a market woman and it was hard work vying for buyers in an open market with even more open prices. The woman with a child on her back stopped at Chika's stall. "It's good pepper. That salt . . ." Chika's chatter stopped as her eyes met the woman's blank stare. There were many like her going through the market, looking for handouts from more fortunate women. The woman stood for a while, saying nothing. Chika slipped some money under a package of salt and pepper, trying not to meet the woman's eyes.

"Thank you." The woman touched her hand lightly. Chika went back to scooping pepper out of the sack.

There were not too many people in the market. Even after six weeks of peace, the distant sound of an airplane still sent everyone scurrying for cover. No one repaired houses or roads and everyone ate as if they were storing food for another war. Detonated distant land mines coupled with the fact that many men had not yet returned from the war delayed the town's return to prewar life.

Especially trying for everyone was the war of the women, which made cowards of local ex-soldiers. The peace soldiers harassed and raped women, threatening the shaky peace without firing any bullets.

Chika finished scooping the pepper, tidied up the display table and started to count her money. That first day, she had run all the way to the house from the achi tree. The door was open. The suitcase she had left for Udo was still on the bed, empty. Everything that was not stolen was destroyed. She was leaving the house when she saw the peace soldier who had greeted her at the achi tree. She stopped, uncertain. He asked her what she was looking for. He was sympathetic, speaking pidgin English with a Northern flavor.

"This is my house," her anger spilled. "Everything is gone. Everything!"

"That's why I am on patrol," he said. "People stealing everything. I help your people. Soldier steal your thing, I kill him!" Chika started to leave. He blocked her way. Gently. Very gently he propelled her back into the house. He spoke softly, explaining what they did as soldiers. It was not only the killing. Sometimes it was about saving lives. The difference was whose lives one saved. Who was friend or enemy?

"Me," he struck his chest, "I friend to all. Me, your friend. Anybody steal your thing, I kill him." His eyes smiled, showing no sign of war or death. His hand over her mouth was gentle; his hold sure and firm. Although she heard him leave, she lay on the bed for a long time, not daring to open her eyes. She was retying her wrapper when she saw the money near the suitcase. That was when she cried as if her heart would break. What had she done? There were four ten-pound notes. Why had she been unable to scream? With shaking hands, she picked up the notes and tied the money in one end of her wrapper. At the market she spent only ten shillings. She walked quickly through the village on her way back to the forest, wondering if the soldier was looking at her.

Chika shivered as she finished counting her money.

"Are you cold?" asked a vaguely familiar voice.

"No."

"How much is your pepper? Is it hot pepper?"

Chika stared blankly.

"Don't you know me?" The thin, hungry-looking man in the Biafran army uniform looked familiar. It was Uche. She shouted her welcome. Laughing and screaming, she catapulted herself from the chair to his side.

He pulled her to him, his hold light, uncertain. Her laughter stopped suddenly, and her face dimmed as the knowledge surged. His unsure embrace, the pain hiding in his voice, his lost right arm.

Camwood

Ulomma wiped her wet hands on her faded yellow dress as she followed her aunt into the front room. Her brown eyes pleaded.

"No, I don't want to do that. Please, Nne, I don't want it like that."

"I think it's the best thing under the circumstances. You're a grown girl now." Her aunt was just as adamant. Her firm voice gave hints of a soprano solo leading the women's midnight music.

"But Nne, I don't want to get married yet." Ulomma stared at the shiny, smooth black-earth floor. If only her life would be that smooth. If only the war would stop. Then Nne would listen to her again. Hear her plans for the future, her life. Since this war settled into their lives, Nne had stopped teaching her as everything became more focused on action. On survival. They had stopped having conversations. These days, Nne mostly gave her instructions. The situation was worsened by the series of deaths of close family members in the last year.

Ulomma missed the old Nne who would spend time talking with her for hours about things that most girls discuss only with their age-mates. This past week Nne's resolve to initiate Ulomma into womanhood was unshakable.

"Your mother would have wanted it that way. Come here." The older woman was calm.

"I don't think that she would have wanted that for me. She wanted me to finish school." Ulomma stepped closer. She averted her eyes but her face was unyielding.

Nne sat down and rearranged her *lappa*. "I know. But that was before the war started. Things are changing fast and no one knows what will happen from one day to the next."

Ulomma studied Nne's lappa as if she was seeing it for the first time. The green birds against the red background on the lappa looked ready to escape into the late afternoon sun. Nne patted her lap, indicating that Ulomma should sit. Seeing Ulomma's hesitation, she said gently, "Sit down, my daughter." Noticing Ulomma's uneasiness at having to sit in her aunt's lap, Nne intoned, "My jewel! My pride!"

To each praise-name, Ulomma answered, "Mm-hmm!" The reluctance in her voice was tempered by the half-smile that lit her eyes.

Nne continued to stroke her with praise-names. Words of praise about Nne's own remembered girlhood filled the room, mixing with a life of memories shared with her niece. Ulomma's spirit mellowed with each memory and she slowly looked up into her aunt's face. Nne was beautiful. Her face was almost heart shaped. Her slender frame reminded Ulomma of palm trees. Her gentle smile seemed to come from a faraway, secure place within her. Even when she was not smiling, her eyes held a smile, making her copper skin look lighter than it was. Again, Nne patted her lap invitingly.

"Sit here. I am still strong enough to hold you, my child."

"I still won't do it," the girl insisted. "I want to finish school."

"Listen." The woman's face set, her jaw thrust out as she looked steadily into Ulomma's face. "I have no more money to send you to school. Your grandfather's burial took the rest of my savings. Besides, there is this war. If we had more time . . ."

"But I have time. I can sell vegetables and *garri*. I can even be the teacher's maid."

"Listen, my daughter." Ulomma relaxed under Nne's warm embrace. These were the only arms she knew. Even when her mother was alive, she lived with Nne, who had no children of her own. Nne was her mother's younger sister, the fifth of six children; three had died in childhood. Nne had married well. Although she was not the first wife, everyone knew that she was her husband's favorite wife. He had brought her back each time she left to her father's compound. So far, he had brought her back three times. He loved Ulomma like his own daughter. He had eight children by his first and third wives. But there was something about Nne that gave a special lift to his steps. With her in his compound, life looked like a good market day when the sun shines without venom. Ulomma wondered what one feels when one is loved like that. Nne's voice brought her back to the present.

"Listen, my daughter. I may not have much time left. Everyone has gone ahead. It's just the two of us. This time last year, my father's house was full of people. I have to do the best I can. Do you hear me? Besides, I do not want you acting like a woman in my house."

Ever since Nne saw her talking to the soldier on her way back from school, Nne had been unusually quiet. She had not said anything until a week ago. Ulomma was not interested in the man. He was a soldier in the Eighty-fifth Battalion, which had taken over the school's dormitories and office buildings. Ulomma did not remember how it started but she had found herself talking with him several times after school. Nne heard about it and the way the other soldiers were said to be looking at her child. Already tongues were wagging about Ulomma's friendliness with shiftless soldiers. Ulomma did not know the extent of Nne's worries until last week, when she announced that Ulomma must leave the win-the-war school. Their relationship had tensed. Both were resolved, but Nne had the authority of both womanhood and motherhood.

Ulomma looked away, withdrawing into herself. "Yes, Nne, I hear you."

"That's good. With all the deaths in our family and the uncertainties of this war, I cannot let you hope that I will be here to take care of you." Nne pulled a knotted red handkerchief from inside her brassiere. The small red ball just fit into her hand.

"Keep this in a safe place." She put the tight red ball in Ulomma's hand. "It is all the savings I have left. We will use it for the ceremony." She stood up, forcing Ulomma to stand within her embrace. Ugo's tall, slim frame blocked out the afternoon sun.

"I am happy that you have agreed. I will go to Ebem-ogo to get a camwood grindstone for you. The oil on a girl's forehead does not last forever." She left, her slight waist swinging rhythmically, asking the world to wait while her feet fearlessly prodded the firmness of the earth. Ulomma smiled in spite of herself. One day, she thought, she too would walk like that.

Ulomma took the red handkerchief into the small bedroom she shared with Nne. She raised the mat and took out a few of the smooth, lightweight slabs of wood. Searching mostly with her hands in the dimly lit room, she found the big iron pot inside the *agodo*. She dropped the handkerchief in it, closed the pot, and put everything back in place. Then she found the kitchen stool and set it in her favorite position, just inside the doorway. From here, she could see over most of the thatched roofs in the compound and still mind her cooking in the back room. She knew the design of every wisp of smoke from the women's kitchens. That heavy blue smoke behind the *aduduo* tree meant that Udo was struggling with her fire.

Udo was her friend. As far as housework was concerned, she seemed not to know her left from her right. Frequently collecting firewood that caught fire slowly if at all, Udo managed to make her mother's kitchen the smokiest in the compound.

As a result, she cooked in the backyard during the dry season. Both girls were seventeen. They went everywhere together. However, the war was slowly ending that. Ulomma would stop going to the win-the-war school. Her age-mates were going to leave her behind. But, Nne said that Ulomma was the one moving forward because no one knew where the war was going. It might last a year or it might last five years. No matter when the war ended, Ulomma knew that school would never be the same again. From Nne's viewpoint, one's girlhood must not be wasted, waiting for others to complete projects like war that had either lethal or indefinite outcomes. Yes, the war would benefit some people, but Nne said that girls in Ulomma's age-group would not be among them. Ulomma's eyes filled with tears again as she remembered the numerous arguments with Nne in the past weeks. She went into the back of the house to get some firewood. As she started the fire for the evening meal, she wondered how people who eat things killed by fire hoped to make peace by killing each other.

Later, Ulomma told Udo that she would no longer attend the school on the hill. Although it was a win-the-war school, the girls loved it. Classes ended early because of air raids. The teachers who taught at the school before the war had all left when the school was shut down at the beginning of the Emergency. Many of the win-the-war teachers were young men and women who were waiting to join the Emergency Army. Some of them worked for the Red Cross or Caritas in the evenings and weekends. Some were university students before the war. They had returned to Biafra from different parts of the country and were teaching for free. For food and shelter, they depended on family members and occasional handouts from relief agencies.

Although the lessons were interesting, the young people found the discussions about the war more exciting. There were many heated debates about whether or not Biafra was ready to be an independent nation. Did all young nations have to experience this much loss, pain, and bloodshed? Before the war, most people had heard shots fired only during the New Yam Festival or at funerals; only a handful had ever seen a live gun. These days gunfire was a normal part of life, and restrictions on travel and refugees with tales of lost relations and property were unpleasant facts.

Ulomma had never seen so many people in the village. However, there was an uncertainty in the air that made it difficult for her to enjoy the new freedom that came with relaxed school rules and the presence of relatives who normally came home for two weeks only once every two or three years. Maybe it had something to do with the fact that many of the returnees came back overwhelmed with grief for lost or dead family members. Maybe it was in their efforts to hide their sadness at the forced homecoming. On the other hand, it could be the joblessness or just the uncertainties of the war and its other unrevealed outcomes.

Ulomma brought out the mortar and pestle. She began to get the condiments ready for Nne to cook the soup. She was pounding the *egusi* when a shadow crossed the doorstep.

"Kpa-kpa-kpa! Is anybody home?" The knocking on the door was soft, the voice was polite.

"Yes, come in." Her friendly voice was guarded. She did not recognize the smiling, well-dressed young man.

"I saw your mother. She said you would be home." He was self-assured.

"Yes." Ulomma was not sure what to do. The young man looked respectable. Was he a university student? A teacher? His evenly spaced pearly teeth gleamed against purple gums. She knew him from a distance. Okwudiri. Yes, that was his name.

"May I sit down? I am blocking the way for your other guests." His manners were pleasant.

"Yes. Sit on this one." Ulomma stood up and gave him the kitchen stool and sat on the mud bed.

"O'dimma." He stretched his long legs comfortably.

"Nne is not here and my brothers went out."

"I know." His hearty laughter filled the room. "I have come to see you."

"Me?" Ulomma looked puzzled.

"Yes, you. I hear you are a very good student. What class are you in?"

"I am in Form Four."

"So you're a senior girl."

"Yes." Ulomma resumed pounding the *egusi*.

"I teach at the secondary school in Obinta."

"I heard that it is a good school."

"Yes, it's a boy's school. What will you do when you finish school?"

"Hmmm. I–I already stopped. I am not going to finish."

"Why? Is something wrong?" He looked meaningfully at her middle.

"No!" Ulomma almost shouted. "No. Nne says we cannot afford it. So I am staying home this year."

"Staying home? Already? Are you old enough for that?

"Yes. My age-group started last year. Besides, my Nne is afraid that she also might die before I get married. This war has changed many things, and . . ." Her voice trailed off.

"Why? Has she been ill?"

"No. This past year alone, my other mother, my real mother, died. Then my grandfather and one of my uncles." Ulomma returned his scrutiny steadily, refusing to blink tear-brimmed eyes in a stranger's presence.

"Chineke forbid a bad thing! All in one year? Is it the war?"

"Yes, all within a year. My uncle died in the North, near the beginning of the Emergency. With him gone, my mother says I should get married. She cannot risk leaving me on my own without a home." Ulomma pushed back the tears with gently fluttered eyelids.

"And who is this that has come to visit us?" The young people started. So engrossed were they in their conversation, they had not heard the older man approach the door. They both stood up, spilling greetings into the late afternoon.

"Nna, this is Okwudiri." The men shook hands.

"Okwudiri?" The older man's eyes narrowed as he tried to remember. "Are you the son of Okwudiri Ibe from Abume?

"Yes. I am his second son."

"Who is your mother, my child?"

"Mgbore Eke from Umuiwe."

"Are you working now?"

"I was at the university before the war. I am a teacher at the win-the-war school for boys at Obinta."

Ulomma tried to slip outside.

"No, my daughter, don't leave. Continue with what you were doing." He motioned to the young man. "Come with me to the otherhouse. My front room doesn't smell of smoke like the women's."

"We'll finish our conversation another time." Okwudiri's voice was barely audible.

Ulomma did not reply. Later, she went to the stream with Udo. When she returned, Nne was making the soup. She did not bring the grindstone. The owner was not home, and Nne had waited for a long time. The woman's neighbors thought she had gone to Nkwo market and would be home later than usual.

They ate quietly in the yellow light of the big hurricane lamp. The soup was just light enough for a warm dry-season night. Later, Nne went to the otherhouse and Ulomma put out the fire and went to sleep.

Several weeks later Nne found a camwood grindstone. The woman in Ebem-ogo never returned from the market. It turned out that she had gone to a distant market two days away. While they were at the market, enemy troops began to shell the town. It was now behind enemy lines. Two other women who went with her came back without their wares or money. They said that people ran in different directions when the shelling started. Despite the uncertainties, a large number of girls were staying home. Ulomma's age-group was large and the war had caused many parents to withdraw their daughters from the win-the-war school. There was no place for unmarried girls in the war. Whether it was the Emergency Army, Mobile Police Force, Red Cross, Caritas, or other war relief agencies, girls were gaining bad reputations because men were in uniform and on the loose. Many of the girls who attended the school on the hill did not have farming or trading skills and were easy targets for the soldiers who hailed from all over the new Biafra.

One by one, the *nzuzu* girls dropped out of the public eye as families redecorated girls' rooms and siblings who previously shared sleeping quarters were moved to new locations. Ulomma moved into the spare room, where Nne kept her valuables. Gradually, the nzuzu girls came to an awareness of their new position in Akasi's nineteen villages. Slowly, they adopted their soon-to-be-women attitudes as they dyed their favorite *lappa* sets in camwood or *ezize*. Brothers, sisters, and cousins who had been playmates could no longer come too close because the red camwood or shiny bronze powder of the ezize would rub off on their clothes or skin.

"Sorry, I can't embrace you," Ulomma learned to say to guests and relatives. Many friends and relatives found out, too late, that camwood did not wash off easily. Some of their clothes would retain the red dye for a long time, announcing to the world that they knew an nzuzu girl. The camwood gave off an inviting, clean, sweet, gentle perfume but it felt dry and powdery to the touch. All the same, close friends asked her to rub off some of the red camwood powder on their arms or legs so that they could show it off. It was a mark of their pride in the fact that they were an intimate part of the process of Ulomma's initiation into womanhood.

Gradually, Ulomma settled into this period of her life when she lived a public life but had more time to think about herself as an individual. It was a difficult time because she had set her heart on going to the university to study journalism. Her friends came to visit her often, bringing news of the vibrant debates about secession, nationhood, and autonomy. She enjoyed their visits with a detachment she would not have thought possible a few months earlier. Udo was her most frequent visitor.

"May I take this pat of camwood?" Udo would ask, prying one off the smooth red-earth wall before Ulomma could reply. Their girlish giggles tickled the late afternoon heat as Udo filled Ulomma in on the latest news from the group of girls whom initiation into womanhood had bypassed for another year.

"Thanks. I'll put it on the soles of my feet. Camwood is said to make them smooth and soft." Udo threw the camwood patty in the air and caught it.

"You'll break it," Ulomma reproached gently. "How was your school today?"

"Oh, it was good. That Matilda is a fool. She couldn't conjugate any of the Latin verbs. The Latin teacher was ready to walk out on us."

"What did she say this time?" Ulomma asked.

"We were doing that *amo, amas* one again. She got as far as *amaggedon!*"

"What? Even I know that one." Ulomma was sorting some pieces of camwood for grinding.

"The teacher says she'll just have to learn it. I don't know what's wrong with some people. Her people are so rich they sleep on paper money. But she can't learn more than a goat can carry in its head." Udo was only half joking.

"What's wrong?" Ulomma asked, sensing Udo's lighthearted bitterness.

"Nothing. I was sent home early. I haven't paid my fees yet."

"Why? What happened? I thought this was a win-the-war school. What do they need the money for?" Feigning indifference, Ulomma picked up the small stone she used as a grinder and began to pound gently at a piece of camwood. She usually pounded the soft red wood into coarse pieces in the evenings. That way, she would not have to make too much noise and attract undue attention to herself in the afternoons when the adults were at the farms or market.

"Maybe they need the money for chalk and other things. My mother says she has no money. She's waiting for her debtors to pay her. Her fish market is not going so well this year because most of the fishermen are now soldiers and the blockades make it difficult to get anything from nearby countries."

"Ask your father to pay for you," Ulomma said, still refusing to look directly at her friend. They both knew the response.

"He still says that school is not for girls," Udo smiled wryly. "Last night he told my mother that I should think about getting married now, as husbands are going to be scarce after the war."

"What will you do?"

"I don't know. It's too late to stay home now. The season is so far gone I'll be as dry as firewood in the harmattan by harvest time. No man will want anything to do with me. They'll think that something's wrong."

"Well, I don't have a suitor yet, either. It doesn't matter that much these days, you know."

"Yours is different. Everyone knows that your Nne is working to maintain your family name."

"Yes. If anything were to happen to her after the ceremony, I'd be a woman on my own, able to negotiate my own terms for a husband."

Neither girl said anything for a while. Ulomma continued to work on the camwood. Grinding camwood was strenuous, detailed work. Although everyone referred to the process as grinding, it required hours of pounding the pieces of red wood, crushing the coarse grinds, and, finally, grinding it into a smooth, wet paste. Like a girl's life, it was difficult at best. And the war was not helping matters. Being a girl was hard work, requiring knowledge of many details that everyone thought you should already know. However, it looked as though most women remembered girlhood as a happy time. It was not clear to Ulomma whether women taught girls to be happy now or taught them to forget how hard it was to be young and female. Some of the boys they had gone to school with were now bat-men in the Emergency Army. Their parents were not afraid they would get pregnant outside marriage or that they would be stranded and unable to get married at the end of the war. In fact, everybody in Biafra was encouraging young men to join the army militia, or BOFF, the freedom fighters unit. Why did the army or an army uniform produce different perceptions about girls and young men of the same age? Even in the middle of this war in which all died equally from bullets and bombs, girls in uniform were perceived as potential harlots while young men in uniform were potential heroes.

Later, Udo left for the stream and Ulomma began to get ready for her trips to the stream with other nzuzu girls. Every morning, before Nne left for the farm, she gave her the names of people on her list for girl-water-gifts. Rarely had she re-peated people's names on the list. Ulomma knew that by har-vest time she would have given water-gifts to most of the women in Oboroji. As Nne went down the list, Ulomma be-came aware of a certain order. Close relations were the very first, then in-laws and their relations, then Nne's age-group, and then the churchwomen . . . Ulomma slipped on her *jigida* one by one over her camwood-dyed lappa. The beads were mostly red, with a few black here and there. Some strings alternated tiny black and red discs. These last few months, Ulomma had learned to start getting dressed on time. Wearing a waist full of jigida was not a job for the careless or hasty. She had learned to be patient and careful with her makeup and dress after one of the jigida broke during her second week. Ulomma had not known that there were so many discs in one jigida. Without saying a word, Nne had rethreaded the jigida.

Today, Ulomma's blouse was a sleeveless, low-cut affair that hardly covered anything. Some of her lappa-blouse sets had lost their original color. Red and dark bronze dominated everything she wore. The gentle fresh scent of camwood and ezize pervaded her room. She filled up the spaces between the jigida, shaking her hips slightly to guess the weight of her gait, of each step. She looked at herself in the mirror on the wall and decided she needed more makeup. She was just finishing with her *tanjele* when she heard her name.

"Are you ready yet? The others are waiting." It was Ola. She was a robust, copper-skinned girl who lived on the other side of Ezi-Ukwu compound. She was always on time.

"I'm almost done. Just a little more of this tanjele, and I'll be there."

She dipped a piece of broomstick in some water, ran the wet stick lightly through the shiny black powder, and applied it to her eyelashes. She snatched her head pad and tiny waterpot from the rafters. There were four girls waiting outside when she stepped out into the late afternoon sunshine. Each had a tiny empty waterpot balanced on her head. Each girl struck a different pose, hands lightly supporting her jigida.

"Ulomma! With eyes that shiny, no one is going to believe all that talk about your family name." Ola was only half joking.

"I think my eyes look pretty. With all this red I need the tanjele, or people will think I'm some mid-afternoon ghost." The girls' laughter brought some children running.

"Look! It's the nzuzu girls!" The children chanted.

"They're on their way to the stream." The children watched, ready to run if the girls tried to catch them and smother them in a red-powder embrace.

"Let's go. The rest are already on their way to the stream."

"Yes, let's go. We want to be home before the women begin returning home from the farms."

The nzuzu girls walked single file. Theirs was the leisurely walk of the surefooted athlete who knows the crowd expects nothing but victory. With both hands holding piles of jigida ever so lightly in place, their eyes straight ahead, not one girl looked as though her head had ever bowed to the vicissitudes of life. Their slender waistlines looked even smaller beneath the red-and-black waist beads. Their youth-filled laughter was thrilling and carefree.

Walking in measured steps, the girls paraded through the compound, crossing the road to the end of the village playground. There they joined other girls who were already waiting. Their girls-going-to-women chatter brought smiles to the faces of the old men sitting under the *achi* tree. Their carefully worded greetings were picked up with pride. Watching the firm hips and protruding breasts brought back memories of bygone days. The old men slapped their thighs and began to tell each other stories of youthful dreams and middle-age lust. As the village fathers, it was their duty to speculate. Those girls they liked would become the wives of their grandchildren and nephews. Unaware or uncaring, the girls shook their waists at younger men, knowing that they had the power of the yes. The road to the stream came alive as the girls began their leisurely descent into the valley.

Ulomma began to like staying home. In between air raids and distant shelling, Nne managed to find all the necessities for an nzuzu girl and some things for a fitting wedding ceremony. For Ulomma the pace was comfortable and Nne's love was sure. Nne told her family, village, and clan history. Sometimes, on days when she had to redo some of Ulomma's braids, the hairdresser came to help. Some days the hairdresser came with another woman. As the hairdresser rebraided Ulomma's hair, the second woman told her some more stories. It seemed as if there was no end to the stories. Ulomma learned fast because she already knew some of the family's and village's stories. There were also many things about becoming a woman that she had to learn—how to start her own small business, who was the best midwife, which families were in charge of different decisions for Oboroji or for Akasi.

"I cannot tell you about your husband's people because we don't know who he is yet. After you meet him, his mother will teach you."

"What if no one wants me?"

"There are ways to deal with that situation. Do you know Mgbechi of Umuiwe?"

"Yes."

"She doesn't have a husband but she has done well for herself. No woman has a bigger market than she has."

"Why are you telling me about land and boundary disputes? I am not a man."

"True, my daughter. That's how it looks. But whether you marry or not, there'll be few richer men. You are my first and only child. Who do you think will get all that land I have acquired?"

"You own land, Nne?"

"Yes, my child. Some of the pieces of land I acquired from bad debts. When people couldn't pay what they owed, I paid for them, and they gave me some land in return."

"Don't they belong to Nna, then?"

"No. Your father has enough land. Besides, what does he want with a woman's land? Mine is all over the place."

"Can't we sell some of the land and get enough money for my schooling?" Ulomma's hope resurfaced.

"No." Nne's tone was firm, resolute. "Nobody exchanges money for land."

"But, you just said . . ."

"Yes. I paid the debts in exchange for the land. No self-respecting person sells land." Ulomma's hopes sank. The question never came up again.

The harvest season was fast approaching. There was still no sign of the war beyond the air raids, the army post on the hill, distant gunfire, continued homecomings from distant lands, the joblessness of those who returned, and the occasional army truck filled with uniformed men who stopped to buy things on market days. Ever since the conversation with Nne about land, Ulomma had decided that her options, for now, were limited. She would go through with the ceremony. She learned to grind perfect camwood, molding the little flat wet cakes and lining them up on her wall to dry. She learned that the quality of the camwood powder was higher the longer she spent at the grindstone. She had time.

She had time to grind her waiting and her sorrows into each wet patty of camwood or ezize. After her bath each morning, she placed one of the dried cakes of camwood into a little bowl. Slowly she would pour water on it until she made a very light red lotion. She rubbed the lotion into her skin. Her skin was now a smooth, glossy brown that glistened in any light. She continued to go to the stream with her friends. She tried to forget her schoolgirl dreams by learning to make her hips swing more seductively.

Sometime into the season, Okwudiri came back to visit. His visits became more frequent. She liked his pleasant smile and easy conversation. He did not say anything about marriage. She thought it would be nice to be a teacher's wife. After the war, he would probably go back to the university. Ulomma's thoughts never went beyond that. She was afraid to make plans about schooling again. Besides, in this war many young men and women were learning to shelve or even kill their dreams and turn to the more practical problem of survival. In addition, they learned songs that put their homeland in new perspectives. Ulomma sang some of them as she ground her camwood. Her favorite had a lilting melody but Ulomma did not know all the words. Udo tried to teach her the words but she preferred only sections of the song.

. . . Our salute to peaceful Onicha; Onicha has food,
Our salute to Aba-ngwa; Aba has a lot of garri.
To Ibiam the leader, the eloquent speaker.
To Police Chief Okeke, the great orator.
Be vigilant about those who roam the land for money;
The world is ashamed of those who will sell the land for money.

New songs filled the land, giving young and old a new appreciation of a heritage that they had taken for granted for so long. To Ulomma it looked as though there was a new song every week. The radio boomed with war news and new songs. Her friendship with Okwudiri, though exciting, was as painfully beautiful as the war songs. He gave her gifts of perfumed soap, pomade, and, once, a necklace. Once he went to Aba and brought back some gold earrings and a nice pair of black shoes, the type girls called *balli*. She told Nne about the visits and showed her each gift. Nne was unmoved.

"What does he want?" she asked. "Do his people know he's coming here?"

"He hasn't said, Nne."

"Don't worry. I'll tell his father to make him stop coming here. Keep your door closed."

"But, Nne, the door has to be open."

"Exactly. But that's not the door I'm talking about."

"Maybe if people knew more about things, they would have had their own children," Ulomma retorted, exasperated by Nne's aloofness.

"You can say whatever you like. But I know what I know. Closed doors keep one's family name open for posterity." Nne left the room in a hurry.

Ulomma could not believe herself. Why had she said such hateful words to her own mother's sister? Ever since Nne decided on this nzuzu business, it was as if an immense wedge had come between them. These days the only real conversations they had were about the village, the land, and Ulomma's future as a woman. She wondered what had happened to their close friendship. Why was Nne so distant these days? Why had her mother died? Why? . . . She went into her room and cried. Later, when Nne came to wake her up for the evening meal, she said she was not hungry. She had a fever and her head felt as if someone was pounding *fufu* inside it. That night the gunfire sounded much closer. Ulomma kept tossing and turning. When she slept, she had a dream about eating fresh fish.

In the morning Nne told Ulomma that the dream was a good sign. Fresh fish in a dream meant that she was fertile and would have many children. Ulomma wondered what having children had to do with the pain in her head and the distant gunfire. Why was becoming an independent nation so difficult? Nne told her to settle down and go to sleep. She cooked some pepper soup for Ulomma before she went to the farm. She seasoned it with *utasi*, just the way Ulomma liked it.

"The tartness of the utasi will reduce the bitterness that the fever leaves in your mouth," she told Ulomma.

She was still in bed when Udo knocked on the door later. Ulomma sat up in bed while they talked.

"You haven't taken a bath yet?" Udo was surprised. Ulomma never missed a morning bath. "Whatever it is must leave you soon. You look different without the camwood."

"What do you mean?"

"Well," Udo surveyed her, "you look, how should I say it? Naked. That's it! You look like you don't have any clothes on."

"What does it matter? I don't think I'll wear any today. How is school since you went to Form Four?"

"It's good. My fees are still not paid completely."

"How much is left?"

"Seven pounds ten. We owe for three terms. It's a lot of money. Every time someone looks at me or says something, I think it's because they know that we owe money. It's so difficult to have your life be so out of reach. My father helped pay for my brothers' schooling, but he won't help with mine." Udo's lips quivered. A large teardrop fell unheeded to the floor. The sun coming through the small window made her dark-brown skin glisten.

"Wait for me here. Don't leave, you hear?" Ulomma left the room. When she came back, she had a red handkerchief tied around something the size of a small orange. Ulomma opened it and counted out seven pounds, ten shillings, which she held out to her friend.

"Take this. Go and pay them."

"Ulomma! Where did you get so much money?" Udo was amazed, fearful. She did not reach out to take the money from Ulomma.

"It's not my money. It belongs to Nne."

"Then I can't take it. She'll kill both of us when she finds out. Her anger is legendary." Udo eyed the money with fascination.

"Take it. She gave it to me. It's the money for the ceremony. I've been saving a yam here and there, some cassava, vegetables, and other things to sell at the market. My cousin Ezera sells them for me. So I've been adding a few shillings every few market weeks since Nne gave me the money, but most of it is hers."

"Then I can't take it. What will you use to pay for the ceremony?"

"You can pay me back when your mother's debtors pay her."

Udo was still hesitant. Gently, Ulomma took her hand and pressed the money into it.

"Take it. One of us has to go to school. Take it, please. Go and pay the fees."

Ulomma counted the rest of the money, wrapped it in the handkerchief, and went to put it away. When she returned, Udo was gone. So she decided to take a bath and eat a little of the pepper soup. The bath was refreshing and Ulomma was singing the latest win-the-war song when she finished. She pulled a lappa around her firm breasts and walked into the front room.

"How are you?" Okwudiri sat on the stool, legs outstretched, self-assured.

Ulomma was too surprised for words. He was wearing a nice blue floral shirt. His trousers looked neatly pressed and fresh. Seeing the neatly dressed young man, Ulomma felt naked.

"Isn't today school?" she finally managed to squeak.

"Yes, it is. One of your cousins told me you were sick. So I thought I should come and see you."

"But what about work? Your teaching?"

"May teaching catch fire. I had to come and see you."

Ulomma tightened her lappa. Her shoulders were still glistening a wet golden brown from the water.

"I have to put on some pomade."

"Wait." He closed the distance between them in two steps. "Won't you at least sit with me for a little?"

"After I put on some pomade and my clothes."

Okwudiri placed his hands on her wet shoulders and tried to pull her to him.

"Listen. When I heard you were sick, I could not do anything else. I had to come. I want you to be my wife. I want to marry you."

"Please, let me get dressed and we will talk. You hear?" She went into her room and started to rub some pomade into her skin.

"That smells like the one I brought for you. Let me see."

"I'm trying to get dressed. Wait." When he would not leave, she picked up the jar and handed it to him. "Here. Take it."

Instead of taking the pomade jar, he took her hand.

4 / *Camwood*

"I love you," he said in English, pulling her to him. She tried to pull away but the lappa came undone and fell to the floor between them.

After he left, she finished rubbing the pomade into her skin. Tears blurred her eyes. There was blood on the mat on her bed. He had not looked back when he left. She did not eat the pepper soup.

When Nne came back, she was still asleep.

"Why didn't you eat? Have you been lying down all day?"

"No, I got up and took a bath."

"Why is your pomade out here?"

"I forgot to put it back."

But Nne was not satisfied. Later that night, after the compound was quiet, she called Ulomma to the front room.

"Sit down." Nne brought the lamp down from the hook where it usually hung every day. She set it down on the floor, letting the yellow light illuminate Ulomma's face. "I want to tell you something." When she finished talking, Ulomma could hardly breathe.

"So, you see, you cannot see Okwudiri again. I went and told his father today. He will tell Okwudiri. You two cannot marry."

"Why didn't you tell me before?" Ulomma was crying quietly.

"Because I thought you would be safe. How was I to know that you'd get sick before the end of the season? You haven't had a headache for years. How was I to know?"

"But are you sure?"

"About what?"

"Are you sure he is my brother?"

"Of course I'm sure. Wasn't I the one who gave birth to you?"

"But why did you give me to your sister and then take me back again?"

"I've told you. I wanted to finish school. I was living with my sister and her husband at Elu-ugwu. Our mother had seven children. She was the first wife. By the time my brother was born, my father already had a first and second son by his other wives. Times were changing fast. And our mother knew she had to find a way for our part of the family to make something of itself. I was the last born and my brothers and sisters did everything for me. They wouldn't even let my feet touch the ground. I used to follow my brother to the mission school on the hill but my father didn't see any use in educating girl children. The teachers said that I was very good at book learning and that I would be a teacher or even a doctor. Our mother sent me to our oldest sister and her husband at Elu-ugwu. He was a court clerk and she worked at the hospital. She and our mother scraped together the money to send me to a girls' school there. My in-law knew the principal of the school so I didn't have to live at school. The other students envied me because I didn't have to answer to all the bells they had to after school. I walked to the school every day and usually stopped at the market to buy some groundnuts or biscuits on my way home. That's how I met Okwudiri's father. He was in petty trading. I went to his store often to buy milk and biscuits. I liked him, but I wanted to go to school. He was already married. I left school. My sister told them at the school that I was very sick. Back then it was not a good thing for a woman to want to get an education. I'm not talking about just getting an education. I mean wanting to be educated. I don't know which was more inappropriate: getting pregnant while still in school or wanting to go to school in the first place. I was a good student, so I wasn't expelled. After you were born, my sister said she would take you so I could go back to school. I wanted to prove that I could do it. My sister agreed with me because she had wanted to go too but never had the opportunity.

"We were too far away from the village, and people there wouldn't know, and my mother's age-mates wouldn't say she and her daughters wanted too much of the new and strange things. With a good education, the bride wealth would be higher and our father wouldn't remind our mother that a girl's education was useless. Our mother didn't like the plan. She wanted me to get married to Okwudiri's father. But times were changing, and I wanted to finish school. Mother agreed to keep my secret on the condition that I didn't come back to the village until after I finished school. A year later I met my husband. He was persistent and I liked him. He gave me many gifts and wouldn't let my feet touch the ground. He had a big store in the lappa and lace section of the market. Besides, as our people say, the palm fruit that falls to the ground has been soiled by the sand. I might never have another chance for marriage. I left school and we had a big wedding ceremony in the town. I started my own trade in provisions. When I couldn't have another child, my sister gave you back to me."

"But why hasn't anyone told me?"

"Many people in Akasi don't know. Elu-ugwu is too far away and many of our people there didn't know about it. Also, because you look more like me, most people could only speculate. We came back to the village after my husband's oldest brother died."

"Does Nna know?"

"Yes. He's always treated you like his child. He too went to school briefly. He liked it but never did too well. Therefore he was quite proud of my book learning and has always supported my trading. I never did much farmwork until this war started. Once, one of his uncles, his mother's brother, asked him if it was true that I had a child before he married me and he told him to mind his own business and not try to destroy other people. We haven't heard anything about it again from him. But that means that his people know. Should anything happen to me, I can't expect them to be responsible for you in things like marriage."

Mother and daughter sat for a while, listening to the story that was unfolding between them. Each looked beyond the yellow circle formed by the lamp into the shadowed darkness, not daring to give voice to the fears lurking there. Outside, that onerous silence peculiar to a war-torn land on nights when there is no gunfire had taken over. On nights like this people called children indoors early and adults who conversed late in their front rooms did so without lamplight. People felt safer when they could hear the gunfire at night because they could tell where the war front was. Ulomma took a deep breath.

"I gave the money to Udo," she said quietly. "She needed it to pay her school fees."

"What money?"

"The money you gave me to keep."

"I don't understand. Do you mean the money for the ceremony?"

"She'll pay it back on time," Ulomma said. Nne did not reply.

They went to bed late. Ulomma could not find the courage to tell Nne what had happened that afternoon. By the end of November, she had missed two periods. She panicked and told Udo to call Okwudiri. For about two weeks, Udo could not find him. When he came, he was wearing an emergency soldier's uniform, spoke in English, and refused to acknowledge Ulomma's pregnancy.

"It could be anybody," he said.

"But you're my brother! You have to help me."

"I know that I should have joined the Emergency Army long ago. Before the war I was a university student. Then, it would have been in bad taste for someone like me to talk to an nzuzu girl. I'm a soldier now, and I don't know why you want to ruin me. However, I'll do the best I can for you. I know an army doctor. He charges seven pounds ten."

Udo brought the money. The day Nne found out, Ulomma was lying in a pool of blood in her room. Carefully molded patties of ezize and camwood were lined up on the red-earth wall, waiting. Nne's grief knew no boundaries. Ulomma died before they arrived at the hospital. Some said it was because they were late finding a car that would take her to the hospital. Others said she was just unlucky. Girls used that doctor all the time.

Broken Lives

As she filled the big earthenware waterpot, Nneoma wondered how her waterpots had survived the war. Except for the floral green *lappa*-and-blouse set she wore, everything was lost. She put the smaller pot in the rafters, adjusted her wrapper, and started to peel a large yam in front of the fire. Her wet, copper-brown skin glistened in the half-light as she prepared breakfast. Her studied movements belied her speed. As usual, she would beat the sun's heat to the farmlands. Her mind's eye raced, making brief stops at moments of hope, faith, or terror in a remembered war whose causes were as uncertain as the present peace. The last cease-fire had brought a late planting season and every day was a rush. This morning at the stream the women were more fidgety than usual, hardly stopping for conversation. A peace soldier's wife had run away from the army camp on the hill.

The day Akasi fell to the Federal troops, Okoro the Soldier-man had told them to leave the town before sundown.

"Listen," Okoro the Soldierman said to Orji. "We are breaking camp. Since yesterday soldiers from the front have been coming into town and the officers are leaving in the good cars. This town will fall in the next day or two. I have worked in the officer's mess for a long time and I know when a town is about to fall to enemy troops."

"I don't know how long you have worked or where but I don't

believe we will surrender." Orji's high voice brought Nneoma running into the living room, where the two men sat. She thought she heard fear, maybe a hint of frustration, in the men's voices and her heart started to pound.

"What's wrong?" she asked. She had plaited her hair the day before and her efforts to contain her anxiety gave her face the dainty composed beauty of the maiden mask.

"They're saying the war is going to end this week. That's what I'm telling Orji. But first the enemy troops will take over Akasi and the remaining Biafran towns." His large brown eyes lacked their usual laughter. "Take your wife out of their way. Go to your house in the distant farmlands. Please, don't tell anybody the war is over. It will be such a big loss after all these years." He stood up and shook Orji's limp hands. "Hurry up and leave before dark, d'you hear? If I don't see you again, please take care of yourselves."

Even now, Nneoma could hear his heavy army boots as he strode off. She remembered his large brown eyes, which were almost always hidden by the soldier's cap he loved to wear. She hoped he survived the war. Okoro was among the first in his hometown to join the Emergency Army. But, according to him, he had yet to see actual combat. His father had begged the recruiting officers to protect his only son because when he was born, a *dibia* had told his mother that Okoro would die young. The dibia had taken his father's money and given Okoro an amulet to protect him from enemy bullets. The recruiting officer took the rest of the money to keep Okoro alive. But the way Okoro saw it, he might as well be dead, working in this battalion where he was used as every officer's batman. Working mostly as a civilian patrol officer in Akasi, part of his job was to organize women and children to fetch firewood and water for the army camp on the hill. Unlike some of the soldiers, he never beat the children with his stick or hit the women with the butt of his gun. The children began to call him Okoro the

Soldierman. Short and heavyset, with a rifle slung across his shoulder, he was a normal part of Akasi's firewood and water patrol, and the children loved him.

Today, weeks after Okoro's early morning visit, the war was over. Everywhere signs of the war hung side by side with the new peace. Dusty, bullet-ridden buildings, a bomb crater in front of the Seventh Day Adventist church, the empty soccer field with its dry red earth and brown grass nursed the leftover fear about tomorrow that Biafrans had acquired during the war. But these were also the signs of their survival, reasons for continuing.

"Are you back from the stream?" Orji's tall form blocked the fragile early morning light in the doorway.

"Yes."

"Yes. Hurry up so we can leave. I want to finish the work in that plot in the Olori farmlands today."

"Can you please sharpen my knife while I finish cooking breakfast? My firewood knife is as blunt as a tongue." Nneoma stoked the fire in the hearth again and started to peel a yam. She did not want Orji to see her anxiety.

"Women," Orji teased as he dipped water for the sharpening stone from the drinking waterpot. "When will you have the sense to keep your knives sharp?" He felt the knife's edge with a finger. "This knife could easily chop off a giraffe's head," he mocked.

"I'll use it to finish off the one waiting at your farm," Nneoma smiled carefully.

"No, I'll make it just sharp enough for peeling yams. That way you won't need the kitchen knife." He was out the door before she could reply and Nneoma breathed a sigh of relief and hurried to prepare a light breakfast of boiled yam with seasoned palm oil. Her mother-in-law had given up trying to convince her to eat something heavier in the morning. Orji also teased Nneoma about her frequent light meals.

"You should have married an office worker," he would say, smiling at her efforts to cope with the demands of farm work on the light fare she loved. "You'll be the poorest woman in this town if you continue eating all the yams in the barn."

"But I like yams. My mother says I didn't eat anything else until I was six years old."

"I keep telling you, I'm not your mother."

"My handsome husband," Nneoma said, "I know that being the good husband you are, you can feed me yams for the next ten years without getting a headache over it."

Before the war, Orji started buying Abakaliki yams so they wouldn't have to worry about not having enough of the stronger local yam seedlings during the planting season. He loved Nneoma. When they got married the year before the war started, Orji was already a wealthy farmer. His father and uncles started a section of yams for him in his father's yam barn when he was very young. Before the national crisis, he already had two barns filled with different kinds of yams and Nneoma was a successful trader in lappas.

As trading became more dangerous and many market women were trapped behind enemy lines, Nneoma stopped her trade to help take care of their farms. Then Orji joined the emergency forces. But he did not stay in the war front for long. A bullet smashed into his side, taking a huge chunk of flesh and exposing his insides. The doctors said they did not understand how he survived. His wound took very long to heal and the doctor sent him home because they needed beds for the newly wounded. When he left the win-the-war hospital in Akasi, his tall, straight form had adjusted into a slight stoop. For the remainder of the war he carried a wounded-in-action pass in the pockets of his fatigue trousers, which had become his badge of honor. He took part in the affairs of the clan and enjoyed his nearly new marriage. Okoro the Soldierman provided him with news from the fronts and the army camp on the hill.

Orji and Nneoma ate quickly and left for the farmlands. Not many people had returned from the forests where the town emptied itself during the last days of the war. So far only the brave and the curious were back to stay. Fear and rumors were rampant. The only sure thing was the brutality of the enemy troops, who had brought soldiers from other countries to help restore peace and unity. Everyone Nneoma and Orji met was in a hurry to continue their journey into the farmlands in the valleys.

"That's how the world is these days," Nneoma said. "No one has the heart to talk. Each one is grieving for something and there is no more trust. Every day another thing will happen. I heard at the stream this morning that Aliezi was taken by the soldiers last night. It's terrible."

"Which Aliezi?" Orji stopped, his deep-set eyes flattening out the worry that struggled to dominate his face.

"Aliezi, the daughter of Nnuola."

"Do you mean Aliezi, the first daughter of Nwizu Okore?"

"That very one." Nneoma took a deep breadth. "A few weeks ago when we were still in Biafra, you think Nwizu Okore would wait for someone to tell him what to do? They say he's sitting at home waiting for the Officer-in-Charge of the peace troops to decide what to do."

"Do you mean Nwizu Okore's daughter?" They had resumed their steady descent into the valley, but Orji's incredulous tone made Nneoma feel they were standing still. She had not expected him to be affected so much by the news. Fear took the seat next to the anxiety in her heart.

Orji was shaken. If Nwizu Okore's daughter was taken and he did nothing, then this thing that had come with the end of the war was great indeed. It was carrying something on its head and hiding more in its armpit. He did not tell Nneoma, but the increasing number of women and girls abducted by the peace soldiers was the reason he went everywhere with her these days.

If Nwizu Okore could do nothing about his daughter, what could he, Orji Ezedibia, already half-dead from the war, do for his wife? Nwizu Okore! The old man with sprinkles of black in his hair who went to the army camp and asked to join the Emergency Army. They thought he was joking and told him he was too old to fight. But Nwizu Okore went back to the army base every day until they recruited him. After two or three war fronts, the younger soldiers, filled with pride about the exploits of the feisty old man with the stately bearing, convinced Nwizu Okore to go home and lead the guerrilla fighters there. Orji could not believe that this was the man waiting to be told how to get his kidnapped daughter back from the peace soldiers.

Orji did not know what he would do if they took Nneoma. Everyone in his family liked her. His three married sisters frequently came to visit her, helping her with work at home and in the farms. She had even convinced his old mother to start drinking tea. Even his taciturn father told Orji to buy Abakaliki yams when he discovered Nneoma loved to eat them.

"Give her what she wants," said the old man, echoing the wisdom of a dibia familiar with the ways of an *ogbanje* child. "Nobody knows what keeps people alive. If yams will keep her here, give her yams."

It was a quiet day and Orji and Nneoma hardly talked to each other once they started working. Exchanging only instructions and comments, they worked without interruption except for a break for the midday meal. Orji seemed merged with his hoe as he made rows and rows of red earth mounds; his supple muscles moved rhythmically as if made only for farm work. He was wearing old khaki shorts and his skin glistened like a new wet penny in the sun. Only the angry gash of the war wound in his side reminded Nneoma why the lilting calls of women moving from one kind of work to another could not be heard. As for the men's booming calls, those had not been heard in the valleys since the number of men began to dwindle at the beginning of the crisis.

As the sun began its descent into the ocean far away, Nneoma and Orji stopped work to find some firewood. The journey back was mostly uphill and slow. At the top of the last hill Nneoma saw a familiar figure.

"Orji, is that your father?"

"Wait here." Orji went ahead and spoke to his father.

"Nneoma, he says you shouldn't go home yet."

"Yes, my child. You should stay in the farms until sundown. I will come here and meet you when it's dark. The soldiers have been taking women to the army camp all day. They say one of the women ran away. They have guns and have already shot and wounded four men from our village."

Nneoma stood still for seven lifetimes.

"What did we do to these people?" She threw the bundle of firewood into the tall grass on the side of the road. Her eyes were bright, dry slits of anger. "We have already surrendered. Why should we live in the forest for the rest of our lives?"

The two men pleaded with her. It was not safe, even here on the road to the farms.

Orji begged, "Please, remember Aliezi. The soldiers took her from her grandmother's kitchen. Nneoma, please. Anger will not help us now. I will go with you."

Aliezi and her two children lived in her father's compound because her husband's house was too close to the army camp. The baby was born during the last week of the war and Aliezi was still bleeding. When the peace soldiers came for Aliezi, Nwizu Okore and his wives were in the farmlands. The soldiers beat his mother and took his daughter. When Nwizu came home, his mother was sitting on the doorstep suckling the baby. Nwizu Okore went to the army camp, but the Officer-in-Charge of the peace troops said he would look into the matter. Now that the hostilities were over, everything had to be settled peacefully. Nwizu went home to wait.

"Yes, I know about Aliezi," Nneoma's voice was little-girl soft. She adjusted her lappa and turned toward the valley.

"I will go back to the farm with you," Orji offered again.

"That is good," said Orji's father. "Wait for me here at dusk." For the next few weeks, they left home at cockcrow and stayed in the farms until late. Orji's father always met them at the same place, his hurricane lamp turned low.

Sometimes, Nneoma's mother-in-law woke her in the middle of the night, whenever heavy army boots were heard outside the compound. On those nights strident, foreign male voices caressed Nneoma's spine with fear, making her wish she could ride the air empty-handed like a witch and disappear into the deep night sky. Each time, Orji's mother guided her to the pit latrine in the back of the house. There they sat on the scrubbed mud floor, breathing the stench of years-old shit. The first night, Ejituru led Nneoma into the valley after the soldiers left and Orji took food to them in the morning.

"I didn't know when you left," Orji said. "They did not search the house."

After that, Nneoma and Ejituru always returned to the house after the soldiers left. Nneoma's parents heard what their in-laws were going through and asked to take her to their house in the distant farmlands.

"No, my in-laws," Orji's father replied. "This is not a good time. Most of the farms are closer to home this year. With everything already late, how will you get your farms ready for planting?"

But they insisted and Nneoma went to stay with her people. She was supposed to stay there for a week but Ejituru took her back after only three nights. The night raids continued. Nneoma's sadness deepened; it was as if the war had not ended.

"Take heart, my daughter," said Ejituru. "This is the war of the women."

Nneoma disagreed. "But we fought the war with everyone else!"

"The peace soldiers don't know that!"

One morning Nneoma woke up with a headache and refused to go to the farm early. She went to the stream to wash some clothes. On the road to the stream, she met Aliezi's father. Nwizu Okore looked old and tired. All his hair was now white, his shoulders stooped. Nneoma talked with him a little.

"Please, my daughter"—he always called her "my daughter" because he was in the same age-group as her father—"don't let them take you too." She promised him she would visit him soon.

Aliezi had decided to stay with the soldiers. That first night the peace soldiers had almost eaten her alive. She didn't know how many of them were there. All she knew was that by morning her bottom felt like a raging fire. Her husband wanted her back. He said he did not care what had happened; she was his wife. Aliezi refused. How could she put that night behind her? She told her mother that she could not go home and live as though nothing happened. When a man takes a woman by force, custom demands propitiation rituals without which the couple would be at risk from ancestral anger and retribution. In this case, asked Aliezi, who did not even know the faces of the assailants, whose names would she take to the ancestors? Nobody knew the answers to Aliezi's questions. No one knew how to console her. Everyone was busy staying alive in the restless peace.

So Aliezi stayed at the army camp on the hill. It was rumored that one of the soldiers wanted to marry her and that she fought with him every night. Her children lived with their father's mother because her own mother could not bear the sight of the girl who looked so much like Aliezi.

Nneoma stayed at the stream most of the day, basking in the sun as she waited for the clothes to dry. She played with some children. She laughed a great deal and spoke to everyone who came to the stream. Later, when people heard that her small waterpot slipped and broke as she reached out to open the door to the kitchen, they concluded she had known all along.

Once she got home her headache came back. She took two Bufferin tablets and began to prepare the evening meal. As she worked, she sang Biafran war songs.

> Take my bullet when I die,
> Oh, Biafra!
> Take my bullet when I die,
> Alleluia, if I have to surrender
> And die forever!
> Biafra, take my bullet when I die!

But her spirits refused to rise with any of the songs she remembered. After the evening meal they sat on the veranda as usual, but Orji's attempts at conversation met with monosyllabic answers. Orji's father was at a meeting. Nwizu Okore stopped by with some news.

"They're saying that the soldiers will leave Akasi tomorrow," he informed them.

"That's good," replied Orji. "That means we will taste the end of the war like other people in this new and One Nigeria."

"You think so?" Nwizu was hopeful.

"Yes," said Orji. "Don't you want them to leave after all they have done to us?"

"No. I wish our ancestors were more active. I don't understand why they are so quiet. If any child of Akasi even thought of any of the abominations these people have committed, the ancestors would strike them with the fire of Kamalu."

"Maybe the ancestors are deaf from the many months of gunfire and bombings," Nneoma joked. She did not want to encourage Nwizu Okore to begin a conversation about Aliezi. "Or maybe they agree with the government that 'To keep Nigeria one is a task that must be done.'"

"Our ancestors are tired. They just don't want to deal with other people and their gods," Orji added.

"I don't know." Nwizu sounded puzzled. "It's almost as if they don't care. I don't understand it. It's as if the ancestors don't care."

They talked with him for a long time. They told him how hurt they were by his loss. It was dark when he left. Sometime in the evening, they heard a few gunshots from the direction of the army camp. Someone said it was probably some soldiers shooting chickens. No one paid attention. Occasional firing was nothing out of the ordinary. Orji and Nneoma fell asleep telling win-the-war stories. Soon after midnight, several shots rang out at the center of the village. Nneoma jumped out of bed and began to get dressed in the dark.

"Where are you going?"

"I don't know."

Orji had his machete in his hand. Soon, there was a loud knock at the door.

"Who is it?" Orji's machete was ready.

"Open the door! It's me." Orji's father came in.

"What is it?" Nneoma asked in a loud whisper.

"It's Nwizu Okore. They say he went to the army camp this evening and killed two soldiers. He tried to take his daughter back by force and they killed them both. Now the soldiers are angry."

"When did he go there?" Orji was astonished. "He was with us this evening."

"He must have gone up there after he left you."

"That must be so," Nneoma said. "He was blaming the ancestors for not doing anything to stop the soldiers."

"I can't say that I blame him," said Orji's father. "This never-ending war. When you think it's over, it brings one more foolishness. Nwizu has been looking for death from the beginning."

Noises of a large crowd came from the center of the village. Ejituru came in fully dressed.

"Let's go!" she said to Nneoma. "Let's go before they come."

"I'll get a lamp from the kitchen." Orji stepped outside. His machete flashed in the full moon, which looked like an overfed child. Orji decided to go back and tell the women that they didn't need a lamp. As he turned, two soldiers, their guns slung over their shoulders, came out of the shadows.

"Who goes there?" one soldier bellowed.

"What do you want?" Orji's voice was raised to warn the others.

"Stop!"

Orji broke into a run. The bullet tore into his side. His machete clattered to the ground. It was the same side the other bullet had hit many months before.

When he woke up, he was lying in a clean bed in the dispensary at the army camp. A woman in a white dress was standing by the bed.

"Thank God! You're awake."

"Who are you?" Orji asked weakly. His head was swimming with pain.

"I'm a nurse. I work with the Peace Army."

"Where am I?"

"You were brought here last night by some men from the town. The Officer-in-Charge said we should dress your wound."

An engine revved up outside. The woman ran to the window and shouted, "Wait for me! Wait!" She turned to Orji. "The wound is not very deep. It won't kill you. The truck is waiting. I don't want to be left behind."

"Wait!" Orji said weakly. "Where's my wife? Where is she?"

"I don't know. There's some water on the table. The truck is leaving!" She ran out to the truck.

Orji tried to get up but the pain was killing his side; the

room reeled and he fell back on the pillow. Later in the afternoon some loud voices woke him up.

"I think they took him with them," said one voice.

"Maybe they didn't. Soldiers are not human beings. They only know how to kill."

Orji began to moan. He wanted to call out but his side was on fire.

"Here he is!" said an astonished, familiar voice.

Orji thought he saw Okoro the Soldierman. Then he fell asleep again.

Two weeks later Orji was sitting in a straight-backed wooden chair on the veranda of the civilian hospital. Okoro the Soldierman sat on a bench, leaning against the dirty, bullet-scarred wall. He had been with Orji every day since they arrived at the hospital in Abiriba. Okoro found a place to stay in the town and visited his friend every day. He told Orji what happened that day of the last cease-fire. The day Akasi fell to the enemy troops.

When Okoro returned to the camp, there were only two trucks left. All the officers had left. One of the trucks was carrying ammunition. The second truck was filled with wounded soldiers. The drivers were waiting for the orderlies to finish helping the wounded and sick soldiers into the second truck. Orji traveled in the truck with the dying and wounded soldiers. As they left Akasi, refugees from nearby towns that had fallen to the peace troops were filling the roads.

Men and women carried children and the elderly on their backs and bundles on their heads. People waved to the trucks, wanting to be picked up.

Okoro said that they passed many towns and he was just beginning to doze off when the leading truck stopped.

"Enemy troops! Enemy troops!" the driver screamed at the top of his voice as he disappeared into the bushes. Okoro's truck stopped and he jumped down from the back of the truck into the arms of a peace soldier. Okoro saluted but the officer was already looking inside the truck. Peace soldiers surrounded the truck.

"Who are these?" the officer asked.

"Disabled soldiers, Sir," Okoro replied, still at attention.

"Where are you going?"

"Breaking camp ahead of enemy troops, Sir."

"At ease!"

"Yes, Sir!"

"Where are you going?"

"Moving ahead of enemy troops, Sir!"

Okoro explained that he was not the only able-bodied soldier riding with the trucks. The drivers were also soldiers and no other vehicles were available.

"There are no more enemy troops," bellowed the one in charge. "The war is over!"

"My brother," Okoro said to Orji, "it was as if someone had poured a bucket of cold water on me. Here I was, standing in the middle of a road, far away from anywhere, and a strange man from a foreign land was telling me that the war was over. One of the wounded men in the truck shrieked, 'Ewoo! Uwa agwula-oo!' I didn't know what to do. Indeed, it seemed as though the world had come to an end and we had gone through those months of hellfire for nothing. The driver sat down in the middle of the road and cried like a child. He called on Amadioha, Kamalu, and Ogwugwu to come and see the end of the world. When the other driver didn't hear any shots, he came out of the bushes. On hearing the news, he went on his knees and started begging the peace soldiers not to kill him. I have never seen anything like it."

When the peace troops understood that they were not in occupied territory, they decided to go back about ten miles to the nearest town. They would not let Okoro and his group locate their battalion. The wounded and sick soldiers received medical attention and food with promises that they would come to no further harm. The war was over. A week later Okoro traveled to his hometown.

"My brother," he said to Orji, "it was like going to another world. Can you imagine that while we were suffering under the blockade in Akasi, my people were living a normal life? I was worried for nothing. My parents are alive and well. My mother was so glad to see me alive she almost killed me with food. Some houses were destroyed when the town fell. Those who stayed after the initial encounter were spared. They even reopened a few schools. But many of our women are now married to the soldiers. Some of them already have children. Many are pregnant."

Orji told him about Aliezi and other women who had encountered similar situations in Akasi after the last cease-fire. Okoro recognized most of the women's names. The men talked about their plans now that the crisis was over. Okoro wanted to start his own business.

"I have always wanted to sell provisions. You know, milk, biscuits, sweets, and other small items." His laughing brown eyes brimmed with life. His soldier's cap sat at angle.

"I am going to build the biggest house in Akasi for Nneoma," Orji vowed. "She deserves some nice things after that war. I will do my best to marry her really well after all this *wahala* is finished." Okoro did not reply. He left soon after.

For three days Okoro did not visit. But Orji was not worried. He and the other patients spent the afternoons telling win-the-war stories and teasing Akuezi, the nurse. She reminded Orji of Nneoma. The other patients agreed that Akuezi's bright face and pleasant voice made life in the hospital a little easier. As usual, those who could get up on their own were sitting on the veranda, avoiding death in the eyes of their companions.

"Orji, your people are here," said one of the men.

The men were sitting on the verandah as usual. A group of well-dressed people was coming toward the hospital building. Orji recognized his mother, his uncles, Okoro, and some members of his family. As they got closer, he saw that Nneoma was not with them.

"You have come?" he called out, trying to get out of the chair.

"Eeeh!" they answered, some of them nodding their heads.

"We have come to see you. How are you?" His mother came up the steps.

"I'm well," said Orji.

"How can you tell her that?" one of his wounded soldier friends asked. "If you say that she'll keep all the good things she brought for us." He turned to Orji's mother and said, "Mma, welcome. How are you? We're not well here. I hope you've come to visit us with a lot of good things that will help us get well." Everyone laughed. After the greetings, most of the patients left Orji with his people.

"Where's Nneoma?" He had hoped someone would tell him without his asking. "Is she well?"

"Yes, she is well," replied one of his uncles, a tall, slender man wearing a traditional george lappa–and-jumper set. Orji's mother nudged him.

Orji asked quickly, "What's the matter?"

"We couldn't come earlier to visit you because we wanted to have something definite to tell you," his mother said.

"That's why Okoro has been here with you," his uncle added.

Orji turned to Okoro. "What's the meaning of this? What are they talking about?"

Okoro cleared his throat and looked at Orji's mother. She nodded encouragingly. Okoro cleared his throat again.

"What's wrong?" Orji gripped the side of the chair and started to get up.

"They took Nneoma," Okoro said in a low voice. Orji's mother started to cry quietly.

"What did you say?" Orji sat down again, his ears ringing with disbelief.

"He said they took your wife," his oldest uncle said. His voice was firm, full of compassion.

"Who took her? What are you saying?" Orji's forehead began to bead with sweat.

"The peace soldiers," said several voices together. Orji's mother was crying loudly now. Some of the patients came back to the veranda. The women started to wail. The veranda filled with sadness, anger, hurt, and the spirit of the suddenly dead caught in the unrelenting world of warring kin.

"What are we going to do?" one of the patients asked. "What kind of world is this? How can a man take another man's wife in broad daylight and nothing happens?"

"Everyone mark it somewhere, this war is not yet over," said another.

Gradually, Orji was told the whole story.

The soldiers took Nneoma the night of Nwizu Okore's death. After Orji fell unconscious, the soldiers took all the women they could find in his father's compound. Later, since there was no other hospital nearby, the men carried Orji to the camp on the hill. The soldiers treated Orji's wounds but refused to give up his wife. The next day they made his mother and the older women fetch water and firewood. When the women returned from the last trip to the stream, the soldiers were gone. They took Nneoma and the other young women with them.

"Two of the women returned." Orji's mother said through her tears.

"They ran away," said one of the women.

"The soldiers stopped to buy some petrol," his mother added.

Okoro's relief was great now that his friend knew the rest of the story. A few days after Okoro saw his own family, he began to worry about his friends in Akasi. He arrived the day the peace soldiers left the camp with the women and convinced Orji's people to send some able-bodied young men with him to the camp. Something told him that Orji would still be there. They found Orji and a few others at the abandoned camp and took them to Abiriba hospital. Orji's father tracked the soldiers down to an army barracks outside Enugu but could find no one there to help him get back his son's wife.

"We've been waiting for your father to come back, but . . ." Okoro did not finish.

"Where is he?" Orji's heart sank.

"He was supposed to come back three days ago. That's why I was away these few days."

"Where is he?" Orji asked again.

"Your uncle came back yesterday from Enugu. They say the Officer-in-Charge detained him for disturbing the peace and abducting an officer's wife." Okoro held his friend's gaze and continued, "Your father saw Nneoma and another woman from Oboroji village in the market. They were buying some yams and refused to return home with him. He paid some young men to carry them from the market. They were trying to put Nneoma and the other woman in a taxi when some soldiers recognized them at the motor park. The soldiers beat them and locked them up."

Orji's mother sent for Okoro when they heard the news.

"We will go and bring your father back tomorrow." Okoro's promise shimmered in the air, merging with the new peace.

Orji nodded his agreement. "Yes. Tomorrow is good."

Children's Day

When they woke up, the sun had brought a beautiful morning but no adults. Uzo turned on the radio. The announcer's drum boomed three times. The flute spilled out eight notes into the dim room. The newscaster was about to read the news. His bright voice greeted in Igbo,

> Children of Biafra,
> Do not sleep!
> One whom enemies surround
> Guards his life at all times!
> . . . The time is eight o'clock!

Uzo turned the radio off. Until this morning, that radio greeting had been exciting. This morning, it frightened him as it echoed through the semidetached house on the outskirts of Owerri Township.

"Leave the radio on," Nnenna said. "I want to listen to the music." She loved radio music. At ten, she knew the lyrics to most of the songs and danced like a palm branch in a gentle rainy-season breeze.

"No," Uzo replied sharply. "We have to find some food. Let's go and look for the key some more." Something in his voice told Nnenna not to continue the conversation. They went in search of the key again, retracing everyone's steps in vain. That key was lost. Finally, they decided to go and buy some food. Everyone put their meager savings on the kitchen floor. Together, they had only enough money for one loaf of bread or two cups of *garri*. They voted to buy some garri. That meant someone had to go to the market.

"We can soak the garri in cold water and put some sugar in it. It will last longer than a loaf of bread and it's more filling," Nnenna reasoned.

Uzo changed into his green shorts. Their deep pockets had no holes, so he wouldn't lose the money like he had lost the key. He preferred going to the market with Mama or Ngozi, the house girl. Their long lists ensured a long trip, a variety of measured conversations with the market women, and some groundnuts or *akara* on the way back. He loved the smell of spices and how the distant humming of the market drew him into its center. He always wondered where the noise disappeared to when he walked into the market. Mama said that it went to his head like palm wine; that was why he loved the market so much. He enjoyed it when the colorfully dressed market women called out, wanting Mama to buy something from them. Some of the women would come out of their stalls, calling to Mama, "Mississi! Mississi! Mek you buy this one! Good fish!" Mama would smile and bargain with them. Sometimes she would buy the fish, pepper, or *ugu*. On those occasions, the women joked with Mama about him. Some called him Little Father, like Mama. Others called him Little Husband. Uzo would hide a little behind Mama, enjoying the attention but not wanting to deal with the women directly. They would laugh and point out to Mama how shy he was, a sure sign that he was well brought up and would go far in life.

Every now and then some of the market women would quarrel over the right to a customer. On those days the women in nearby stalls would join in. Some would try to stop the war of words while others would take sides. And, Chineke-God!

the things that came out of their mouths! He was always amazed at how these women who spoke nicely to Mama or teased him about his would-be wife could turn into such lionesses. One minute they were speaking in pleasant, sonorous tones, the next they were throwing abuses at each other, their words simultaneously smelly and enticing like ripe oranges rotting in the hot sun at the foot of an orange tree.

"Today you will tell me if your father owns this market!"

"Isn't your mother that one they say never stays home?"

"If you call my mother's name one more time, I'll show you whose mother has no husband! Bush animal!"

"Look who's calling someone 'bush'! When was the last time you saw soap?"

By now those not directly involved would try to calm the combatants. Most of the time their intervention worked, because the women would be threatened with fines for disturbing the peace. But some days there would be retyings of headties and *lappa*s and someone would place herself between the would-be lionesses to prevent a full-fledged physical fight. Depending on the situation, Mama would make some placatory noises in the back of her throat and say to no one in particular, "That's enough, biko," or take Uzo away from the scene.

Today, Uzo wondered what he would do if some of the market women were in a fighting mood. It was a hot morning and he was hungry. Already his white shirt was sticking to his back and his dark-brown face glistened with sweat. He walked slowly behind Iheoma. At eight, she was rambunctious, full of life. She went everywhere with him and loved to play soccer with him and his friends. Uzo would be unable to protect her if anything happened at the market. So, although it cost more, Uzo bought some garri from the women without stalls, who sell their wares at the edge of the market. He used some of the change to buy some groundnuts for Ofor. He felt better as they turned homeward.

They walked slowly. Alone in the house for the past two days, the children had exhausted their favorite games. Even Iheoma's inexhaustible energy supply was waning. And Uzo refused to acknowledge the question in her wide, innocent brown eyes. His twelve-year-old mind raced ahead to the time when their parents would come home and answer Iheoma's questions. But only his fear was real.

The war was getting closer and Mama went to prepare the house in the village. Everyone said that the war was coming to Owerri and people were secretly packing their belongings. Talking about it meant you were afraid of the war, or worse, a saboteur. So Uzo was not supposed to tell anybody why Mama went to the village. Some of his friends had already returned to their villages in more remote parts of Biafra. Mama said that since the village was not as busy as the township, the war would not go there. Papa, a medical doctor in the emergency forces, sent word last week that he was coming home for a few days. But he had not given a date for his arrival and the anxiety was eating up Uzo's imagination.

Nnenna and Ofor were waiting on the veranda. There was no sign of Mama or Papa. Nobody. Uzo's stomach tightened. Again, the radio announcer's voice rang in his ears:

> Children of Biafra,
> Be vigilant!
> One whom enemies surround . . .

But in his heart was the now nagging question, Where is Mama? He continued to walk toward the veranda, determined not to be afraid.

"We didn't go into the market," Iheoma reported as soon as they were within earshot.

"Uzo, what happened? You said that you know the way to the big market."

"We bought some garri from the women at the edge of the market." Uzo was defensive.

"You were afraid?" Nneoma accused. Uzo looked away. The tears stung his eyes; his ears tingled.

"There's some sugar on the table," Iheoma interrupted. "Let's eat."

"Shut up, you silly girl. You're always thinking about your stomach!"

"I'll tell Mama when she comes back."

"Stop it, you two." Uzo placed himself between the girls to stop them from fighting. They did not see Ofor go inside the house.

"Why are you two always fighting?"

"We're not!"

"Then let's go inside. Ofor and Iheoma need a bath."

"I don't want to take a bath. I'm hungry. I'm going to tell Auntie Monica that you two won't give us any food," Iheoma said.

"No, you can't! Mama said not to tell anyone where she went." Uzo grabbed at her dress as she stepped off the veranda.

"Where did she go?" asked a cheery, familiar voice.

"Ng-o-o-o-zzzi-i-i!" The children's shouted greetings could be heard down the road. They ran toward the girl, almost knocking her over in their excitement. She was about sixteen years old, long limbed, with beautiful, smooth ebony skin. She wore a knee-length light-green cotton print skirt with a matching sleeveless blouse. The skirt was lightly gathered at the waist.

"Don't tell me you missed me. Iheoma, you're covered with dust! You were wearing this dress when I left on Sunday." She was laughing as she tried to untangle herself from their embraces. Uzo took her bag.

"Why is everyone outside? Where's Mama? Where's everybody?"

"We don't know."

"Where did you go?" Iheoma asked. "We've been so-o-o hungry. And Uzo was afraid."

"And you were not afraid?" Ngozi wiped the sweat from Iheoma's face with the hem of her skirt.

"Where's Mama?" She had lived with the Okafors for three years. Mrs. Okafor let Ngozi take sewing lessons in the afternoons. Ngozi called her Mama, like the children. She said that one day Ngozi would own a sewing shop, get married, and have a big house.

"She went to the village," Nnenna replied.

"Where did you go?" Iheoma insisted.

"I went to Enugu to visit my big sister." The children followed as Ngozi led the way into the house. Everyone was talking at once and Iheoma held so tightly to Ngozi's waist, she could barely walk. Uzo set Ngozi's bag down in a corner of the kitchen. It took a while for Ngozi to understand that Mrs. Okafor was not home and that the children did not know when she would return.

"How is your sister?" Nnenna asked.

"I didn't get there until Monday. When I arrived there was nobody in their yard. Some of the doors were open but the rooms were empty. I tried to find my sister and her family. But you could hear enemy fire as if it was in the next street. People were leaving town. Most didn't know where they were going or if they even wanted to leave. There were cars and lorries everywhere. People on foot with their belongings in big head bundles. Some had wheelbarrows. There were children crying for their parents. I didn't know where to look for my sister. I didn't even find anyone who knew them. I left Enugu on Monday night. I was going to walk back to Owerri because I didn't have enough money for the taxi back to Owerri. Some people gave me a lift to Okigwe. I took a mammy wagon into town this morning." As she spoke, Ngozi filled the kettle with water and lit the stove.

"So you have actually seen the war?" Uzo asked. The respect in his voice was unmistakable. Ngozi smiled. Everyone knew of Uzo's excitement about the war. So far he had seen nothing beyond uniformed soldiers on drill.

"Not exactly. I ran away from it." Ngozi finished tending the stove. "Where's the key to the fridge?"

"It's in Mama's room," Nnenna said, avoiding Uzo's eyes.

"Where's the key to the room then?" She poured some garri into a bowl.

"It's lost." Uzo fixed his eyes on the floor.

"When did Mama leave?" Ngozi's eyes narrowed, her brows creased with concern.

"On Tuesday morning," said Uzo and Nnenna together.

"So you've not eaten," Ngozi summed up the situation. "Where's Ofor?" In the excitement of Ngozi's return, they had not noticed his absence. They looked at each other blankly and then ran in different directions shouting his name. A few minutes later, Iheoma found him. He had the empty sugar bowl in his hand.

"Chineke-Nna! Ofor, did you eat all the sugar?"

"Yes," Ofor said, the laughter tinkling from deep inside his belly. He looked happy with himself.

"Mama is going to kill me." Ngozi looked in his mouth, willing the sugar to come spewing out.

"We were going to use that sugar to eat the garri," Iheoma said.

"You will eat something else. Leave him alone!" Ngozi yelled as Iheoma lunged for Ofor.

"Uzo! Nnenna! Go and wash up. Ofor, come. I'll give you a bath."

"What about me? What should I do?" Iheoma asked.

"I'll give you a bath later. Put some garri in this other bowl." Ngozi took a small bowl from the cupboard. "Soak it in some water. Here's some salt."

Iheoma sniffled as she soaked the garri. She hated garri with salt and water.

Later, as they sat at the dining table eating the last of the garri and listening to stories of Ngozi's adventures, they heard a rumbling, as of distant thunder. Ngozi held up a hand. "Wait! Listen!"

"It's Ogbunigwe." Uzo was unperturbed. Loud explosions in the distance were part of the war and everyone was used to hearing them any time of the day or night.

"No! Wait! It was a different kind of noise."

Before they could make up their minds, the earthbound thunder rumbled again. This time it was closer. Uzo ran to the window.

"Chineke-umu-Izrel! No! It's a bomber! Everybody, take cover. Uzo! Come back here." Ngozi's voice was drowned by a low-flying bomber. Nnenna hid under the table as another bomb exploded nearby. Ofor began to cry and Iheoma attached herself again to Ngozi's waist. Ngozi was sweating.

"Quick! Close all the windows!" The older children rushed to shut out the blossoming chaos outside. Soon it was clear that closed windows could not shut out the raging, screeching flying boats. There had been other air raids. But none had ever sounded this close. Today one of the bombers had decided to make its return swoops close by.

"Has the war come?" Uzo's excitement was tinged with fear.

"I don't know." Ngozi held back the tears. She had not told the children the whole story. Mama had told her that she could no longer afford to pay her. Schools had been closed for a long time and Mama, a secondary school teacher, was no longer working. She had told Ngozi to go back to her people. But first Ngozi had to notify her sister, Ugoeze. That was the plan when she came to live with them.

"Tell Ugoeze I'll bring you back next week." War or no war, Mrs. Okafor was going to take Ngozi home herself.

"Yes, Ma." Ngozi was upset.

"I promise I'll come for you after the war," Mrs. Okafor tried to soothe her with words.

Ngozi was heartbroken. When she couldn't locate Ugoeze, Ngozi returned, hoping that Mrs. Okafor would let her stay until she found her people. But Mrs. Okafor decided to go to the village after she sent Ngozi to Enugu and Ngozi did not know what to do. With the Okafors she was sure of food, shelter, and adult protection. Today it looked as if the war was here and she was in charge of the children. Ngozi huddled with the children on the kitchen floor, waiting for the bomber to leave.

Later she went to Auntie Monica to explain their situation. Auntie Monica gave her a big bowl of *jelof*-rice and some yam. That evening Auntie Monica went to the Okafors' home. Her shiny copper-brown skin overshadowed her fading yellow blouse and old, plain george lappa. Her nice plump body reminded one of new brides.

Udochi had not returned. Monica Irohara swallowed her fears and sat Ofor in her lap. Although her husband had joined the emergency forces, he was stationed at an army base a few miles away. He was an NCO and the supplies manager at the base. Although Monica saw him often, she understood the pain of separation the Okafors felt. A medical doctor, Ikenna Okafor was commissioned early in the Emergency. Udochi often shared with Monica her fears about his constant exposure to active combat as he went from one war front to the other tending the wounded.

Monica joked with the children. They made up possible reunion scenes with her friend, their mother. By the time Monica left, they were sure that their mother would return the following morning. And she told them that they were always welcome at her house. That night Ofor began to vomit. He was sick all night and the children, remembering the air raid, were afraid to take him to Auntie Monica. During the early hours of the morning, he fell asleep.

When they woke up it was late morning. There was still no news of Mrs. Okafor. Although people traveled from one part of Biafra to the other, communication was ineffective and people mostly lived fragmented lives in which they hoped for the best by the hour. War fronts had proliferated and there were no post offices, telephones, or even reliable human contact. At sixteen, Ngozi already knew that life was hazardous at best. Worried about her new role as head of household within the family that had taken her in to help show her a way to a decent adult existence, she went to Auntie Monica's again. She wanted to tell her about Ofor. He needed his mother. But Mrs. Irohara's children told Ngozi that a relation had come from their hometown with some bad news the night before. Auntie Monica had left for the village at daybreak. Her younger brother who had joined the emergency forces had died in action.

Ngozi decided to go in search of Mrs. Okafor herself. She would take the children. They had had a rough time these past few days. She told them to get ready to go to Abiriba, their hometown. If their mother wasn't there, the extended family would take them. Ngozi hoped it would not come to that. But she could not forget her own frustrating search for her family earlier in the week. She went to the post office and withdrew all her savings. It wasn't much but if they took the mammy wagon, she could pay their fares to Abiriba. From Umuahia they would board another mammy wagon to Abiriba.

She packed a few clothes for everyone and they were soon seated in the back of an old mammy wagon bound for Umuahia. Passengers sat close together, their feet resting on bulky indeterminate bundles, baskets full of yams, plantains, and other market products piled on the floor of the truck. The conductor joked with the market women. He was nice and didn't take any money for Ofor's fare. So Ofor sat in her lap eating some groundnuts she bought from a hawker. He looked a little tired. The air was heavy with the smell of sweat and heat. Filled beyond its capacity, the truck wobbled a little, trailing a red-brown cloud from the dust that always covered the tarmac. The children talked excitedly about seeing their mother and the extended family again. Comfortable in Ngozi's lap, Ofor soon went to sleep. Ngozi was beginning to doze off when the truck sputtered to a stop. The passengers were told that the engine only needed a little water; they would be on their way soon. But it was nearly two years into the war and engine parts were strung together with wires, twine, or whatever scraps vehicle owners could find. In many cases even those were hard to come by. But resourceful Biafrans had learned to rebuild almost anything, becoming more creative as the war progressed. The conductor pulled out a five-gallon water can from the second-class compartment and poured some into the engine. But the truck refused to start. He pulled and adjusted some of the engine parts. He talked to the engine, calling it "my broda" and begging it to start just one more time. But the engine remained deaf to his pleas.

Finally, the driver and the conductor went off to consult in whispers with each other. One by one, people got off the truck. The women, familiar with the uncertainties of wartime travel, spread their lappas on the dusty grass and sat down to wait. The driver assured everyone that there was no problem; he and his conductor would repair the engine soon. The Okafor children amused themselves by guessing the makes of approaching cars and the origins of their license numbers. Two other children joined them from the second-class compartment.

Ngozi leaned against the truck. Its orange paint was beginning to peel. Like all mammy wagons, this one bore its owner's philosophical views about the world. Ngozi stood back to read it. She was surprised at its simplicity: God Dey. Ngozi hoped that whoever had written that knew what he was talking about. She looked around. The truck's engine had failed in the middle of nowhere. Here the forest was thick and green. The women said that the nearest town was miles away. Before the war many people would have attempted the trek. But the forests of Igboland had become hostile. It would be foolhardy to attempt walking unarmed anywhere these days. Some of the women said they could smell fresh water but no one wanted to look for it. Those who had water bottles shared with others.

After a while the driver told them that the conductor would stay with the passengers while he went back to Owerri to find a mechanic. People asked for their money back. But the driver got angry and told them to wait for his return. He'd be back soon, and how did they expect him to pay the mechanic?

Some of the passengers decided to forfeit their fares and flagged down cars or trucks. The drivers took advantage of them because it was late in the day and they were stranded. Listening to some of the men as they bargained with the driver, Ngozi's hopes fell.

"If you no wan' pay, mek you walker reach Umuahia."

"I beg, my broda! Na just from here to there now!"

"Com'ot for road! Bloody fool. You no fit buy tire sef. If na from here to there, mek you walker!" The driver would rev up his engine, covering them in a shroud of red dust. Ngozi knew that if she paid another full fare to Umuahia from here, they would not have enough money for the fare to Abiriba. One man, who had only a briefcase, was lucky enough to get a lift from a family in a small car. He could barely squeeze into the back seat.

The market women with their baskets and bundles of perishable foodstuffs could not find room in any passing vehicles. The mammy wagons were full; the taxis would not even consider the women's baskets. The women began to sing wartime songs.

3

We all agreed with Ojukwu on One Biafra,
We all agreed with Ojukwu on One Biafra!
When it got rough, the weak and afraid went to Nigeria.
Oh! Oh! Where is my child?
Ebelebe!
Nsukka sector, where is my child?
Oh! Oh! Where is my child?
Ebelebe!
Onitsha sector, where is my child?

One of the women, Mama Flora, became the lead singer. A vivacious dark-skinned woman with a huge gap in her front teeth, she was a natural leader. Her dark red lappa-and-blouse set with a blue head tie only further accentuated her dignified manners. Ngozi wondered what she had done for a living before the war. Mama Flora called out the names of big and small towns in Biafra. The tune was sad, almost a dirge. But not quite. It was a cross between a war song and a funeral song. It didn't matter that some of the cities mentioned had been won back from the front lines or had never even been war fronts. What mattered here, in the middle of road in Biafra, was that everywhere was a potential war front. Everywhere people were dying from the war. Anytown, Biafra, was a war front in its own right as Biafra's children died from starvation, illnesses without names, and just plain desperation about violated or lost childhoods.

The Okafor children joined in the singing. Soon they were suggesting marching songs from their school bands. The women helped move the music along, changing some words and embellishing the tunes. That evening, the men told stories about war and loss. They told of families separated and fortunes lost, of the food days before the war. Their stories were about Affia-attack—those risky trading trips across firing lines. They told stories about the luxury-padded lives of people on the Nigerian side. About families subsisting on next to nothing until the women returned from their trips with much-needed onions, salt, dried fish, and aspirin. About the simple pleasure of seeing a starving child sleeping for hours after a full meal. The women shared their groundnuts, saltless akara, and other goodies with the children and other passengers.

"You should keep some for your children," Uzo suggested to Mama Flora.

"Today, you are my children. I'll buy some for them tomorrow," Mama Flora replied. "Here, let me hold that one for you. He's a big boy." She took Ofor from Ngozi and tried to feed him some akara, but he wouldn't eat.

"But we're not your children," Iheoma countered.

"You will understand it later, my daughter. Biafra's children are all from one mother. When we understand that, we will win this war." Mama Flora retied her lappa. She passed around the remainder of the conductor's water. The next morning, more people left in other vehicles bound for Umuahia or Owerri. The driver returned around nine o'clock with a mechanic. By early afternoon the engine revved up again. At the Umuahia motor park, Mama Flora helped Ngozi find a taxi going to Abiriba. She was from a nearby village and didn't mind waiting for the young people to leave.

"I have a daughter your age. She's in the UK with some friends. I was on leave from my job. I came home for a short visit just before the borders closed. I've tried everything but I've been unable to go back there or bring her home." She wiped her face with the end of her lappa. "You shouldn't be out in this war by yourself. Especially with a child this young." She touched Ofor's cheeks. His face crinkled with laughter.

"Be careful. They're saying that the war is on its way there."

"But the war can't be there yet." Uzo was dismayed. "It hasn't reached all the big towns yet."

"I don't know, my son. I don't know the ways of the war. All I know is what I hear on the radio." She retied her lappa for emphasis, her lips pursed determinedly. "Be careful," she said to Ngozi again.

"Yes, Ma. Thank you, Ma." Ngozi pulled Ofor closer as the taxi started to leave the motor park. It was an old blue Peugeot station wagon. Iheoma, Nnenna, and a heavyset man shared the middle seats with her. The red seats were torn. Uzo and two men sat in the back while the driver and two other people sat in front. Soon they were on the outskirts of town. But Uzo couldn't recognize the landmarks.

"Where are you going? This is not the way to our hometown."

"We have to take a less-used road," one of the men sitting next to him informed him. He was a tall, dignified-looking man with distinctive eyebrows and well-groomed hair. His clothes, though dusty, were well made. He wore dark sunglasses. The driver said nothing.

"What happened to the other road?"

"It's not used much anymore. Many of the towns along the river are now war fronts. The other road is closed."

"Are you saying that the war has reached here already?" Uzo's voice trembled a little.

"On and off," the man said. "It's difficult to tell which towns. Sometimes our men take a few back. The most difficult are the roads. Keeping them open and safe even in peacetime should be at the top of our national agenda."

"I hope the war hasn't come to our hometown." Iheoma turned a tear-streamed face to the man in the sunglasses.

"Don't cry, my child. You should keep your eyes clear of tears. That way you can help us make sure we don't drive into an ambush."

Uzo gasped. "But we don't know anything about war. We live in Owerri."

"Owerri is Biafra, my child. Many men have fought hard to keep it safe. Without places like Owerri, Onitsha, Umuahia, Orlu, and Aba, we have no Biafra."

"What of Enugu?" Iheoma did not want Ngozi's hometown left out.

"Enugu is very important," the man assured her. "It was the capital of the then East Central State. All the important government offices are there. Its people are industrious. Onitsha is a peaceful town. Sitting on the great River Niger, it provides plenty of food for us. Aba is important for garri, Biafra's staple food."

"We ate some garri today," Iheoma said.

"Yes. Most people eat garri every day. That's why our farmers must be protected. The farms must be cultivated, the crops harvested. Safe, healthy farmers make for a healthy nation."

"Are you a soldier?" Uzo asked. The man seemed to know so much.

"Sssh-sh-sh!" Ngozi turned to him, a finger to her lips. "He's an army officer. Can't you see?"

"But he's not wearing his uniform," Nnenna said.

The man smiled. The driver looked into the rearview mirror. Ngozi saw his eyebrows lift slightly as his eyes seemed to meet those of the man. She looked at him again. He looked familiar but she couldn't quite place him.

"The woman said that you are going to Abiriba." It was a question.

"Yes, Sir," Ngozi replied.

"Driver!"

"Sir!"

"You should go to Ohafia first. Then come back from the other side."

"Yes, Sir."

He sounded self-assured. For the first time in days, Ngozi felt safe. Whoever the man was, she was glad he was in this taxi with them. The driver, too, was good. Either he had the eyes of a cat or he knew this road like the back of his hand. Although darkness had descended on the rolling hills, every so often the driver would turn off the headlights.

"We don't want enemy scouts to see our lights. They're either on the hilltops or in the valleys. It's easier to hide in places like that," the driver told the children. The station wagon clung to the hillsides like a child to its mother's back. Sometimes the car was barely crawling. After the two passengers in the front seat disembarked at Ohafia, Uzo wanted to move to the front. But the man in the sunglasses placed a firm hand on his shoulder.

"Stay here. It's late."

Ngozi moved to the front seat with Ofor, who was sleeping again. Ngozi thought he had a slight temperature but she wasn't sure. Soon he would be with his mother. Between Ohafia and Abiriba the hills were steep, the valleys deep. As the car dipped into a valley the driver turned off the headlights and swerved into the bush. Ofor slipped from Ngozi's grasp and crashed headfirst into the windshield. Ngozi screamed.

"What happened?" someone asked.

The men in the back seat were on the ground in a flash. The driver had hit his chest against the steering wheel but was still breathing. Ofor's little body was still. Ngozi tried to breathe life back into him.

"He's gone. Give him to me," said the man in the sunglasses.

When they drove into Abiriba it was almost midnight. The second man in the back seat drove the rest of the way. Ngozi returned to her seat. The driver sat in the passenger's seat, showing the way. The man in the sunglasses in the back seat held the baby. His bowed head, supported in one hand, made him look as if he was protecting the child. He couldn't bring himself to look at his brother. Watchmen from the villages stopped them every few hundred yards. But they knew the driver and allowed the station wagon to pass the checkpoints without much conversation. Finally the driver and the kind gentleman took them to their front door. It took the driver almost ten minutes to convince those inside the house to open the door. Someone brought a hurricane lamp but was told to take it back inside.

"You'll attract enemy gunfire."

"Do you want to kill us all?"

"Where's Mama?" Iheoma asked over and over.

Finally, Mrs. Okafor came out. She almost fainted when she saw the children.

"Ngozi! How did you get here? We were cut off three days ago. We are behind enemy lines."

"That driver brought us," Uzo said.

"How did he do it? Your father was almost killed. He came in yesterday. Where's Ofor?"

Ngozi's cry rent the night air. The man in the sunglasses came out of the car and gave the cold little body to Mrs. Okafor. Quickly, quietly, the front of the house filled with keening women. Children, stretching from interrupted sleep, began to cry. The station wagon drove off into the night.

"Mama, why didn't you come back?"

"Mama, he was sick. I wanted to bring him to you." Someone led Ngozi into the house.

"Mama, I was afraid. Ofor is dead. Mama, I don't like the war," Uzo cried as if his heart would break.

"Who was that man?" asked one of the young guards from the last checkpoint. He had followed the car into the compound.

"Which man? The driver? That's Omenka," someone replied.

"No, the one with the baby. I think it was the major general," the young man said. But no one knew for certain who the man was. They began to get ready for the morning.

Ogbanje Father

In twenty-five years, Akuma and his wives buried eleven children. He consoled himself with the fact that they still had seven. As a youth he had had dreams of a large bustling compound, filled with children's laughter, the sound of small hands playing clapping games, and small feet running to hide behind the big *aduduo* tree during a moonlit-night game of hide-and-seek. He saw himself working hard during the planting season, tending huge plots of yams during the rainy season. He imagined his wives' rows of corn waving in the wind amid wide leaves of okro and cocoyams. He saw himself coming home from the farm and saying to one of his many healthy children, "You! Come here. Take these peppers to your mother. Hurry! Tell her they're from her pepper bush near the palm tree at Olori." That was a lifetime ago. Before this war collided with his dreams.

Back then he was tall, and lanky, with a strong right arm. His prospects for cultivating many plots of farmland were high. He was handsome. People said that the dark-blue *nki* marks on his red-brown cheeks complemented his pearly white teeth and wide forehead. Straight of bearing and supple-backed, he danced like the whip of the *okonko*, the masquerade of the Ekpe secret society. In those days, no young men's dance group in his village was complete without him. Men reveled in his ability to respond to the language of drums, and women wondered about the strength in his loins. Everyone knew he would have many children. He did. He was popularly known as Nna-Ikoro, after the first child he had with Ogori, his first wife. Ikoro lived to the ripe old age of seven. He woke up one morning with a stomachache. By the end of the following day he was dead. Many years later Akuma and Ogori were still recovering from the suddenness of that loss. After Ikoro, the children continued to die early. Some died as infants; all died before the age of seven. Often he would look over the head of a vibrant child at Ogori, his eyes holding a prayer, begging her to believe one more time in their ability to continue a homestead. Over the years he married four wives. But his children were said to be *uke-mmuo* or *ogbanje*—spirit-children, who, in keeping with promises made to their age-mates in the other world, could come only as sightseers, tourists to the world of the living.

He married again after Enyaeru, his second wife, died. Enyaeru's three children now lived with Ogori, who had two living children. People told Ogori to leave him but she stood by him through the years. She alone knew how he was suffering from the losses. These days, with war raging through the land, it was even harder. Akuma was now the oldest male in the compound and the only one among his age-mates who had no son in the Emergency Army. Before the war, he consoled himself by teaching the young men a dance he had made up as a young man. He called it Adigh-r'Igbo. Every year he added new steps to the dance and everyone agreed that there was no dance like it in all of Igboland. All but a few of those young men had joined the army. Those who had not joined the army worked for various win-the-war efforts. Whenever Akuma saw them in their uniforms a big lump of sadness settled in his chest. He knew that by the time his one son grew to be their age, he, Akuma, would be dead.

Still people talked. Some said that *ndi-ichie*, the ancestors, had cursed his compound. Others said the curse was from Obasi, the ancestral god of war, who watched over Akasi from the shores of the big river. No one knew exactly what Akuma did to deserve ancestral wrath. But how could he dispute it when his children kept dying? The last burial, two market weeks ago, was especially painful because he had become used to the joy of having Egwuatu. Born early in the war, Egwuatu looked very much like Ikoro. The thought that Ikoro had come back had helped stem Akuma's fears about the ongoing war. Surely, if the gods had decided to grant him a son during the war, it was a good sign at a time when others were losing grown sons. For two years Egwuatu looked strong and healthy. His death left Akuma inconsolable.

Last planting season his fourth wife, Iguola, joined one of the new churches after his eleventh child, her first, died. For the past four days she had been trying to convince him to join the new church. Last night he told her he would think about it. She was pregnant again and they were praying for her at the church. She said that her church leader could cast out evil. They talked far into the night. Before the war it was possible to take a sick child or relative to the hospital in Aro. However, the war had taken most of the doctors to the war front. The hospital was a shell of its old self, and many people had returned to the native doctors while others began to develop a new belief in the power of certain individuals who were said to be holy.

Overnight new sects sprang up across the war-torn land. Akuma did not know what to think. He was too old to join the army and not educated enough to be part of the new leadership. He had never been much of a churchgoer. Even as a child he had gone to church grudgingly. Then he had found ways to miss church, even though it was required by the headmaster, who used church attendance to decide when a student would go to the next class. However, the new mode of worship did not satisfy Akuma's artistic spirit, and the wooden benches were hard on his buttocks.

"What if while trying to cast out the evil thing, he casts out my *chi* with it?" Akuma said.

"If it is your chi that is behind this, don't you think you are better off without him?"

"Nobody is better off without his chi; a bad chi is better than none."

"Just come to our church and Leader will tell us what is wrong."

"I know what is wrong. My children die early. Their age-mates in the spirit world do not want them to stay here too long. If Leader can find a way to talk to them . . ."

"So you will go with me." It was a question.

"What will I tell the others?"

"My cowives?"

"Yes."

"Tell them that you are now a churchperson."

"Will the churchpeople be here when my in-laws come to ask me to return their daughters' bridewealth?"

"Do you want bridewealth or? . . ."

"It's not about bridewealth," Akuma interrupted. "It's about Ogori and Erimma. I don't want them to think that I have gone to church and left them on their own."

"Then ask them to come, too."

Akuma sighed. "You don't understand. A man must not do certain things. It would be madness to leave my compound in search of some impossible cure."

"But they also want you to go."

"What are you talking about?"

"Why do you think I'm here tonight? In my condition, I should be asleep by now."

"You mean? . . ."

"It's true." Iguola did not let him complete the question. As the silence stretched into the darkness around them, she took a deep breath. "It's true," she said again. An explosion rumbled at a nearby war front. Instantly, a chilling hush engulfed the night outside, making the husband and wife feel totally exposed to a power beyond their control.

"That war seems to be coming closer every day," Iguola whispered, inching closer to Akuma while trying not to disturb the frightened night.

Now, in the sanity of the late-morning light, Akuma ate his fu-fu with hot aduduo soup slowly and wondered if he could fulfill a promise prompted by the uncertainties of night. It was a mild day and he could hear the distant humming of Afor-Ebi market. The occasional car horn hinted how busy the market had become over the war years. Three of his daughters sat on the smooth cement floor, waiting for him to finish eating so they could return the dishes to Iguola. The children liked Iguola's aduduo soup and she always gave them some more food to eat if they agreed to wash the plates.

"Did you go to the stream today?" he asked the children.

"Yes. And we bathed ourselves too," piped Orie, the youngest girl, who was about seven years old. Apart from occasional attacks of unexplainable fevers that left her weak and the whole family helpless, Orie was a vibrant, happy child. Everyone loved her irresistible laugh, which seemed to come from around rather than inside her. Of the remaining children, it was she Akuma was most afraid of losing. Akuma smiled. Orie's dark-brown face shone, proof of the amount of Vaseline she had used to oil her skin after her bath at the stream.

"Nna, are you going to give us some fish from your soup?" she asked.

"Yes. But wait until I finish. It's not right to leave good soup like this naked."

The girls laughed. "How can your soup be naked, Nna? It's not wearing any clothes," Orie said.

"He means there'll be nothing left in it," said the oldest girl. "It is difficult to eat when there's nothing to bump against your fingers every now and then. Right, Nna?"

Akuma nodded. "An empty soup and a big mound of fu-fu means that one is greedy." As he looked at the children, the pain of all the other losses swept over him. What if the church leader did not know what to do? And if Leader were successful, would Akuma be allowed to keep the children saved by the church? Was Iguola right? Although she had not lived long in his household, he wanted to believe her. Iguola was a fighter. She was much younger than his other wives and wanted her own child badly. It took him a long time to convince her to marry him. She said he was too old and refused to even talk to him for months. However, the more she said no to his advances, the more Akuma liked her. He admired her smooth, shiny brown skin, the big gap between her front teeth. She had a joy for life he knew would lighten the weight that death had put in his compound.

"Nnaa-wo!" It was Nwankwo, his only brother.

"Nnaa-wo! Come in. You have met me well."

Nwankwo pulled up a low kitchen stool, washed his hands, and started to eat before replying.

"I am glad you have not finished eating. Ugo and the children went to the farm to get some pumpkin leaves for the market. I just came back from inspecting some traps. How are the children?"

"They are well. What did you catch?"

"Nothing. Mother says you should not go to that church."

"Who told her I am going anywhere?"

"I'm only telling you what she said."

"I've made up my mind. I will go." Akuma was more surprised than his brother was to hear the announcement.

"That's good."

"What do you mean?"

"It's good. I am also worried about the children. If going to the church will help, then go."

"But people will say that Iguola is leading me."

"They are already saying that. The children are important. Our people say that only the madman knows his own mind."

The men finished eating and washed their hands. After sharing the fish their father left in the soup bowl, the children took the dishes back to Iguola's kitchen, chewing happily.

"The land dispute case with Amaachi will go to the court soon. The letter came yesterday and I have been asked to represent Odigga," Akuma informed his brother.

"I hope you know what you are doing. Those Amaachi people like trouble. They'll try something when they find out who's going to Elu-ugwu."

"Don't worry. I can look after myself. Everyone in Odigga knows there is no Amaachi man I can't beat in a fight."

"Yes, but they might not be planning to fight face to face."

"I'll be ready for that too."

Nwankwo stood up. He adjusted his *lappa* and straightened the big white shirt over it. He did not want an early-morning quarrel with his brother. Akuma was his older brother and known for not changing his mind once it was made up. He rarely took anyone's advice, and it took a great deal to make him see some things. He did not understand that in the village he needed a different kind of vigilance than he was used to in the township.

"I will see you at the meeting in the village square." Nwankwo strode away, swinging his walking stick. Nwankwo's walking stick lent his walk a certain dignity. He started using a walking stick soon after he first got married. Just for style, he said. He bought the stick on a whim at Ito market and had used the same one for years. It was a simple stick, unadorned and with a curved handle. Over the years, many Odigga men had tried using a walking stick the way he did. But none had quite achieved Nwankwo's flair and elegance. It had to do with the way he seemed to lean on the stick while swinging it. Each swing was followed by a well-measured planting back on the ground in a rhythm understood only while he was within view. Even Akuma had given up trying to understand it.

Later that afternoon, Akuma said to one of the children, "Tell your mother I have gone to Ime-ezi."

Ime-ezi was the main compound where the rest of Akuma's family lived. Akuma's house was on the outskirts of the village on a piece of land that had served as the women's vegetable garden for generations. The large zinc-roofed house occupied an extensive portion of the land bordering on Amaachi land. The *umunna*, his kinsmen, had given him that piece of land on his return from the big city after his father died. Becoming part of the umunna again had been difficult after many years' absence. Although Akuma's presence and services as the first son were required, Nwankwo had occupied the main house in the compound so long that everyone thought that Akuma should build another one. As soon as the umunna agreed, he built his new house on planting ground. Although most of the land was still used as vegetable gardens, Akuma's new house prompted the umunna to divide the remaining land into potential residential portions. Since one of the boundaries with Amaachi was already under dispute, many families began to lay foundation stones for new residences. Some began to build but the women continued to plant their vegetables and the occasional cassava plot. Some of the gardens blossomed inside unfinished rooms flanked by waist-high walls green with moss.

Akuma's years in the township were good. He had made a good living as a petty trader. There, each of his wives had a stall in the township market. Since his return, he had immersed himself in village life. He took the appropriate titles and joined the two secret societies for men and not much happened in Odigga without his knowledge.

The humming of the market got louder, becoming distinct conversations as he approached the village square, where the market had moved since the war started. A small crowd was clustered around a group of dancing Odigga women who had heard about the letter and were celebrating the imminent defeat of Amaachi in the boundary dispute case. As Akuma got closer he was able to hear the women's song more clearly.

> We all agreed with Ojukwu on One Biafra,
> When the time came, the cowards among us ran away.
> Oh! Oh! Where is my son?
> Ebelebe!
> Nsukka sector, where is my son?
> Oh! Oh! Where is my son?
> Ebelebe!
> Benin sector, where did my husband go?
> Oh! Oh! Where is my husband?
> Ebelebe!

It was an impromptu gathering. There were no drums, ankle bells, or gongs. The women were in their market clothes. The dance itself was not the usual energetic dance of market women. The dance circle was fluid as women joined in or left to go back to their wares. One of the onlookers told Akuma that the dancers had just changed the dance steps from those of victory to ones of mourning. Their feet hardly left the ground as they danced, barely raising any dust. Akuma watched the dancers for a few minutes and went on to Ime-ezi. Nenne was sitting outside when he entered the compound.

She called out the familiar greeting, "Whose child is good-looking? . . ."

"And his mother does not smile?" Akuma's response to the customary exchange was automatic. Some of the older men and women in the compound called out the praise-name that had set him apart during his days as the leader of young men's dances.

"Your mother went to the back of the house. How are people in your house?"

"Everyone was well when I left."

Nenne was his father's grandmother. Although his mother was still alive, Nenne was the main reason he went to Ime-ezi so often. She came from a family known for its longevity. Her delight in the artistic was legendary. And among the best-known loves of her life was Akuma.

"How is our youngest wife?"

Although he was expecting the question, Akuma almost missed it. Sometimes it was almost as if his grandmother spoke a different language. Two rows of beautiful tiny blue-black nki marks ran from her forehead down her chin, disappearing into her printed red blouse. She told him long ago that when she was young, nki marks were a mark of both female beauty and strength. A young woman who could withstand the pain of the incisions was sure to do great things in life. As though in testimony, Nenne's well-aged copper-brown skin still glowed with health. Akuma always marveled at the beauty of this old woman, whose physical and spiritual strength seemed to come from a different time and place.

"She is well. I have decided to go to that church. They say that the leader is a great seer. Maybe he will help us keep the children."

"Keep which children?" Nenne's voice had a hint of augury.

"Our children." Akuma was impatient. Why was Nenne talking as if she did not understand?

Nenne laughed. She sounded like one of those spirits said to inhabit masquerades.

"Akuma, son of Okore Akuma!" The old woman's eyes shone like distant stars on a clear night. "Who told you that those children are yours to keep? How can you keep things that are already gone? Answer me that!"

"They came to us. Why shouldn't they stay?"

"You want to ask your chi why he has made your life the way it is?" She pointed toward the path he had just come from. "Have you also asked your wives' chi?"

"What is it? Nenne, why are you talking like that?" Neither of them saw Akuma's mother return from the back of the house. "Whose son is good-looking? . . . How are my children?" She greeted.

"Everyone is well."

"Nenne, what is it?"

"It's nothing," said Akuma and Nenne together.

"Whose chi are you supposed to have confronted?" Ota ignored their pointed denial of the argument they were having when she walked in. "What have you done?" The eyes she turned to Akuma were insistent.

"He has joined those churchpeople. He left his good trade in the township and came here to join I-don't-know-what. Now he wants them to tell him where the children are."

As Nenne spoke, Ota ritually circled her head with her hands, snapping her fingers at the end of each circle. It was a ritual denial of what she saw as impending abomination by her son. After the third circle was completed and broken, she asked him, "Is that true? Did you come back from the big town to bring shame on us?"

"All I know is that I am joining them. Iguola said that . . ."

"Iguola! Iguola said this. Iguola said that! Is that all you ever say these days?" Ota's voice rose to wailing pitch.

"Don't do that!" Nenne's firm voice diminished Ota's wailing to sniffles. "He's not dead yet."

"Are you saying that Iguola's chi is stronger than yours?"

"No, Nenne," Akuma answered, as though the question came from his grandmother. "There is a seer there. He sees more than Okari-uke, the *dibia*. Iguola thinks he can help us."

At the mention of Okari-uke, Nenne's face changed. Over the years, Okari-uke had taken everything he could from her and her family. But Okari-uke, whose feats with the spirits were well known throughout Akasi's nineteen villages, remained powerless against this affliction to her family.

"When are you going?" Nenne took a deep breath.

"I'll go this evening after the meeting of the elders."

"Do they meet every day?"

"Tomorrow is Sunday. But I am going today to meet that leader."

Nenne seemed satisfied for the time being. Ota's sniffling stopped. They skirted around the issue a little more before the conversation changed to the land dispute with Amaachi and the court case.

After the meeting at the village square, Akuma went to the church. It was a solitary long building in the middle of the tall grass. The women had painted the outside walls with white-wash and floral borders drawn in charcoal. Some attempts had been made to weed the area immediately around the building. But the grass was already growing again in the clumps of red earth thrown haphazardly around the building. Akuma went inside. It was a long room with a few backless benches arranged in two rows. A candle was burning on a table at the far end of the room.

"Welcome, my broda," a man's voice said from shadows beyond the circle of light created by the candle.

"Ndeewo!" Akuma replied.

"You must be our new person, Mr. Akuma Okore." The man moved into the light and down the aisle between the rows of benches. Even in the half-light, Akuma could see that he bore his height well.

"Yes."

The leader was dressed in a long white robe. He wore a pointed hat, also made of white cloth. He had a Bible under his arm. When he was close enough, Akuma extended his hand. The leader looked pointedly at his outstretched hand before looking disinterestedly toward the door behind him.

"There will be no handshaking on the day of judgment," he said. Then he turned around, motioning Akuma to follow him toward the lone candle. "This is the table of the Lord," said the leader. Beyond the flickering candlelight was total darkness. The table was covered with a nice old-fashioned george lappa.

"We are all called to the table by the Redeemer. Wetin bring you to our church, my broda?" The leader switched to pidgin English. Although Akuma understood him, he did not know what to say back in pidgin. He had stopped going to school after Standard Two and had not spoken any English for many years. In the township, most people spoke pidgin. Also, since he became a member of the group of elders and increased his participation in the soul of the village, he had not spoken the language of the newly educated for a long time. He strained into his recent past for words: "I no know."

"My broda. Make you no shame. This na prayer house."

"I have never been to this kind of place before. Iguola, my wife, said that you would tell me what to do," Akuma said in Igbo.

"What would you like us to do for you?" the leader asked in Igbo, lightly scornful of this man who refused to show off his knowledge of the new times.

"I am looking for answers about the children."

"What have they done?"

"Nothing. They have done nothing."

"We cannot do anything unless we know what you want."

"They die. That's all."

"Do they die from headaches, stomachaches, poison?"

"No."

"Is it enemies, friends, or neighbors?"

"No. They just die. In the morning, afternoon, or night. They die."

"Too much cold or too much fever?"

"No."

"They just die?" The leader sounded unsure. This was a new situation. Usually people made his job easier by suggesting the direction he should go. For example, it was easier to convince the woman who suspected her cowife of trying to usurp conjugal privileges to put her faith in the Redeemer, the one husband who could not fail her. A man who suspected his wife of adultery could become convinced into looking again at the possibility of vibrant relationships after he learned how to keep her in check. Ukaegbu had no formal training as a church-person, let alone as a church leader. He had a mortal fear of killing anything and had started the church as a way of avoiding conscription into the Emergency Army. Because of the war, he had acquired a more than decent following. Akuma's problems posed a new threat—that of exposure. Ukaegbu took the book from under his arm and closed his eyes. He held the book toward the candle and intoned in English.

"Father of all! This is Akuma! He has come to ask for help. Help him!" He opened his eyes and said to Akuma in Igbo, "This is the big book, the holy book of the church. Before it you must not tell a lie." He closed his eyes again and began to talk very fast in pidgin. Very soon Ukaegbu's prayer became a mixture of pidgin, Igbo, and phrases from around the world.

"God! Oga! Mek you help us! Help dis broda! Him pikin dey die. Him no get more pikin again. I no know wetin mek you do, but if you fit helep am, mek you helep am. The man sef, na ol' man. Him no fit mek new pikin again. Glory! Glory! Halleluya! If you no helep am, I no go fit chop today. So, oga, God, mek you come quick quick! Olorun! Abasi! Olodumare! Amadioha! Mek you no forget us. We be your pikin wey want pikin! You come like tif in de night. Domine, Nomine, e-supiri-supiri! Halleluya! Halleluya! In God we trust. Sanu, Allah! Halleluya!" As the leader's voice rose, he began to tap one foot. Then he began to sway slowly. Finally he put the book carefully on the table and began to shake as one in the grip of a great fever.

Akuma stepped back to give him more room. Soon, Ukaegbu's words became unintelligible. Beads of sweat fell from his forehead as his gyrations took him in a circle dance several times around the table. Suddenly he stopped and looked toward the open door into the new darkness outside. Without changing his voice, he pointed to Akuma and said in Igbo, "You must come here for seven days. The same time. You should bring your wife Iguola with you. Both of you must be dressed in white. Bring two white candles." There was a pause. Akuma tried to say something but the leader held up his hand.

"That's all." Although he was still breathing hard from his recent exertions, he was otherwise fully composed. "You have to leave now. I have to pray about your case. May the day break!"

"Wait! But you just told me what to do."

"I don't know yet what to tell you, my father. Your case is a difficult one." Ukaegbu sounded uninterested.

"But you just told me to come here for seven days."

"No."

"You said I should bring my wife and we should come in white clothes." Akuma was almost begging.

"That must have been the Holy Spirit. I was only praying for guidance." Ukaegbu sighed with relief.

"Then listen to the Holy Spirit. Let us see what he has to say."

"I can only go by what Chineke wants. If that is what you heard, then that's what we must do."

"I heard you clearly. It must have been the Holy Spirit," he said with admiration and wonder. "We shall come tomorrow."

"May you and your family sleep well."

Akuma went out into the new darkness. There were two elders in his front room when he got home.

"We have come to ask you to go to Elu-ugwu with us," said one of the men after the initial greetings.

"What happened?"

"We received a letter from the court. They want someone to answer some questions at Elu-ugwu."

Akuma thought about the leader. "Does it have to be tomorrow?"

"We were supposed to be there last month. Their letter was late."

"We need you to come with us because you know the big town more than any of us."

"You should take a younger man who knows their language. I can't put my tongue around it. It's too fast for me," said Akuma, remembering a place with a lit candle and encircling darkness.

"We will invite a younger man to go with us for the hearing."

"When are we leaving?"

"We'll take the first mammy wagon. It leaves around five, right after they ring the prayer bell at the mission."

After the men left, Akuma told Iguola what happened at the church.

"We must go as soon as possible." Iguola's voice could not conceal a familiar dread.

"What happened?"

"Orie is ill. Her body is burning up with fever."

"Where is she? Where is Erimma?"

"She took her to Nenne. She has nursed Orie back to health before."

"Tell Leader we will be there the day after tomorrow. I'll be back by evening."

"I will tell him."

It was another week before they met with the leader again. The mammy wagon had engine trouble and the delegation spent days on the road. Their journey was futile. Parts of the road to Elu-ugwu were behind enemy lines. After a few days of not knowing what to do, they met one of the younger men from Akuma's dance troupe who had a pass to go home for a short leave from his battalion. He suggested that the men should go to the court at Umuahia. The court clerk there told them that the court was open only occasionally when the judge came back from the war front. He told them that they should have read the letter well. It said they were expected the month before at Elu-ugwu. But, the elders asked, how were they supposed to know what to do when the letter itself was late? The man gave them a date for the following month. He said they should come then to see if this judge would hear the case. When the men returned to Akasi, Orie was still with Nenne, who kept her on a constant dose of the special brew of herbs she used for reducing fevers. The gunfire from the war front sounded nearer than usual. Rather than the usual distant, almost indifferent staccato of the drums of amateurs, it was beginning to create consistent echoes of fear in the heart.

That evening, Akuma, filled with a familiar fear, went with Iguola to the church. The leader was waiting. As soon as he saw them, he said that their lateness might cause some problems. He had told them to come for seven days following the first meeting. Where had they been? He told them that he had lost some of his special focus on their case because of their reluctance to come back to the church. They begged him to do what he could. They haggled with him for a while, promising to double his charges for their kind of request. Finally, Ukaegbu agreed to continue working with them after they promised to take to his house a basketful of yams, ten cups of rice, some stockfish, salt, and pepper. That night his prayer was longer, his dance more animated. When he finished, he laid his hands on their heads and informed them that he had to conduct an official ceremony to bring Akuma into the church. He had to become a member of the Children of the Light Church.

"Tomorrow we will have a castin'-and-bindin'. You will become one of us."

"What is castin' a'bandin'?" asked Akuma.

"It means we will take you out of the reach of the Evil One and make you a follower of the real Chineke. We will throw all your bad luck away. Come here tomorrow morning."

On their way to the church the following day, they met Okari-uke, the medicine man. When he saw Akuma and Iguola, he stepped off the path, facing the bushes as they passed him. Iguola almost ran the rest of the way to the church. At the door she stumbled into Ukaegbu, who was standing just inside the threshold.

"Welcome! Welcome, my broda and sista," he said, motioning them not to enter further. "I have to wash your feet before you go inside."

A large earthenware pot sat on the floor, almost blocking the entrance. It was filled with water. On each side of the pot were an egg and a chicken feather. The couple exchanged glances. Akuma stepped back into the open. As a titled man, he could not, without purpose, cross what was obviously a boundary between men and spirits.

"First, I shall wash you clean with this water. The eggs will be broken in front of the building as you enter."

"But you said this is your house of prayer? . . ." Akuma was angry.

"You speak the truth, my broda."

"Where is this water from?"

"It is the water-of-God."

"I mean, where did you get it from?"

"It is water from Amaachi stream. The only pure stream in Akasi."

Akuma gasped. "You! Your mother is from Amaachi, isn't she?"

"Yes. And so is my grandmother, the sister of Okari-uke's mother."

Before Iguola could raise an alarm, two strong men picked her up while four others surrounded Akuma. They carried them into a windowless room behind the table with the flickering candle. There was a small Vono bed, a table, and a chair in the room. A big hurricane lamp hung from a wire suspended from a beam in the low thatched roof. A curtain of plain red cloth hid the rest of the room from view.

"Okari-uke is waiting outside. If you settle with us, he will not smear you with his medicine, which is guaranteed to make you stark raving mad."

"What do you want?" Akuma could barely contain his rage.

"We want you to stop the court case. The land is ours."

"How can I stop it while you're holding me hostage?"

"We will let you go. Your wife will come home after we hear from you and your umunna."

"No! You must not agree to this, my husband. Let them kill me today! What am I saying? They have already killed me!" Iguola's scream merged into a call for help from Okari-uke. The Amaachi men scrambled for the door behind the red curtain. At the same time, the door crashed to the floor, pulling the curtain with it, and big strong Odigga men, brandishing huge sticks and machetes, ran in. For a while, there was a great deal of grunts, thuds, crashes, and muffled cries as the men fought.

Later, Okari-uke, Leader, and two Amaachi men were carried to the hospital. The only casualty on the Odigga side was Nwankwo, Akuma's brother. He had gone to confront Ukaegbu. When he arrived, the fighting was already in progress inside the building. An Amaachi man, taking advantage of Nwankwo's unwariness, snatched his walking stick from him and hit him over the head several times with it. Nwankwo died before the army doctor agreed to treat the wounded men, four days later.

The soldiers refused to give permission for the firing of the customary gun salutes befitting titled men's funerals. They said it was not a good idea to fire guns when a war front was so near. There were no local young men at the army barracks and no one could convince the soldiers, who were from other parts of the new nation.

The funeral was hasty, quiet, and bitter. Odigga men were ready to go to war with Amaachi, and emergency soldiers had

to be brought in to settle a few fistfights. The soldiers repri-
manded the elders for fighting over irrelevant issues. They
told the fighting elders to go to the front if they wanted to see
war. They hit some of the elders with the butts of their guns
and locked them up in the barracks for a few days for the sake
of peace.

After three market weeks of difficult negotiations, Amaachi
elders sent a peaceful delegation to Odigga. The delegation
said that Amaachi elders had no hand in what had happened
and agreed to give up Amaachi's claims to the land. That evening, news came that the Biafrans had fought bravely at the
nearby warfront. The enemy troops had retreated. Once more,
the gunfire was like distant, foreign drum sounds announcing
the threats to other people's lives. Nenne went to visit Akuma.
As was his practice since Nwankwo's death, he was sitting,
chin in hand, alone in his front room. He blamed himself every
day for what had happened to his brother.

"Whose child is good-looking? . . ." Nenne greeted as she
neared his house.

"And his mother does not smile?" voices chimed in from
around the new compound.

"You! Bring a chair for your Nenne!" Akuma said to no one
in particular. Orie, vibrant with life, brought a chair for Nenne
and sat down on the floor at her feet.

"I have come to see you," she said as Akuma came into the
room.

He offered her some kola.

Nenne rearranged her lappa and took a bite of her kola.
"Did your wives tell you what happened?"

"What happened where?" Akuma asked.

"You mean they haven't told you the whole story yet?"

"I don't know, Nenne. Which story?" Akuma frowned.

"You have people, my son. That day you went to Elu-ugwu,
Ogori overheard some Amaachi men talking to the driver of

the mammy wagon. They told him he was the son of an Amaachi woman and should know what to do. Ogori was going to the stream. She hid behind some bushes in order to hear more. She says she saw Okari-uke talking to the men. They told Okari-uke and Leader that if they were successful, Amaachi elders would convince the army officers to remove Okari-uke's son from the war front. When you did not come back after one market week, we thought they had killed all of you on the way to Elu-ugwu. After you returned safely, we knew that it had to do with the churchpeople. Your wives (you still have people, my son!) told every Odigga woman to tell her husband to be ready for a big fight.

"That morning, some of the young men from your dance group hid in the bushes near the church. They saw Okari-uke deliver a medicine pot, eggs, and chicken feathers to the leader and sent a message back to warn you, but you had already left. One of the children told Ogori. She alerted the men. Nwankwo had gone to his traps and heard the news from one of his children when he returned. He decided to confront Okari-uke at the church. He said that once you saw him, you would know the situation was serious."

"But we did not see our men. They hid in the bushes until the last minute," Akuma said.

"Nna, who brought eggs?" Orie asked. For the first time, Akuma noticed the new nki marks on her cheeks and forehead. The razor-sharp wounds had healed well, leaving tiny blue marks.

"My child, I don't know." The marks looked unfamiliar, alien on Orie's smooth, young skin.

"Nna, will you buy some eggs for me?"

Akuma looked at Nenne, a question at the tip of his tongue. A distant spate of gunfire caused him to stop. Nenne nodded, eyebrows slightly raised. Her nki marks flickered, like so many stars marching in place, from her wrinkled forehead down to her chin and disappearing down the bodice of her yellow print blouse. Akuma leaned back in his chair and turned to look at Orie again. Slowly he crossed his arms over his chest as though he were trying to hold his heart inside his body.

"Yes," said Akuma, nodding his head.

"Yes, my child." He smiled broadly, looking at his daughter as if for the first time.

Relief Duty

She pulled out the sandals from under the bed with her foot. They were her last pair and the straps were broken. They had been pretty sandals when she first bought them almost three years before. After constant use for the past two years, the only recognizable thing about them was the fact that they had once been brown. She shoved her slender feet into them, tied the light-green scarf on her head, shut and locked the door, and tucked the key inside her bra. She walked quickly, shuffling slightly because of the strapless sandals. Soon she arrived at the relief office, where she worked.

"Good afternoon, Money."

"Afternoon, Mr. Eze."

"Sort the stockfish. The different medicines are already in the box over there. The sacks of cornmeal are in the back of Father's car."

"Yes, Sir!" Money's face was without expression as she started the sorting. She went to the cluttered table in the back, pulled some heavy sacks from under it, and began to put pieces of stockfish in them. The stockfish had already been cut. She put the heads in one sack, tails in the next, and the middle parts in the last. It was easier to arrange them like that. It helped the relief workers distribute them more quickly. It also reduced quarrels among the recipients. Many people liked the head of the stockfish because they said they could taste it more in the food; without salt any taste helped one swallow the food more readily. Others were more particular and grumbled if they didn't get substantial pieces of stockfish and salt. This late in the crisis, Money and the other workers made sure they kept everybody satisfied, because people's morale was low.

Usually this part of her job didn't take long. But today there was a large pile.

"Are we expecting a larger-than-usual crowd today?"

"Yes. Hurry up, Money. We have to be at the village square in less than half an hour." He left, almost tripping over the two steps outside.

Today, Mr. Eze was grumpier than usual. Money took a deep breath and concentrated on the sorting. She would have liked to know why Mr. Eze thought there would be more people than usual, but she decided not to upset him more than he was already. She was not from these parts. She had been working at the relief office for only about three months. Her real name was Monica. In the secondary school, she had run the 440 race for the school. Her classmates had shortened her name to Moni. Later, it became Money because she always won the race. In Form Four, she started writing her name as Money in her textbooks. When they filled out the forms for the school certificate examination, she had gone home to see her brother Solomon, who had to have his appendix taken out. Someone had filled in her name as Money Ukaegbu. She found out just before the exams and went to the principal to correct it, but he told her that the name had already been submitted to the examination board and corrections would not make it to the board in time for the change to be effective. Besides, everyone already knew her as Money. Although some of them knew that her middle name was Iheoma, officially Money became her name. When the examination results came out, her certificate bore the new name. She paid the newspapers to change her name in those change-of-name ads. From then on, all previous documents remained valid, and she went to the Advanced Teacher Training College known as Money to everyone.

She was in her last year at the teacher training college when the war broke out. Without the National Certificate of Education, she was unable to get a good-paying job in the Emergency. Her fiancé, who was among the first few to join the emergency forces, died within the first few months. In her hometown near Ihiala, people rumored that she was ill-fated, and men refused to seek her hand in marriage. In a situation where many were already confused about the nature of the forces behind the war, she decided to make the best of her life and wait for the war to end. She joined some women in Affia-attack, the petty trading across enemy lines, to help her parents' meager income from the farm. Affia-attack was risky business. The traders crossed enemy lines and went to market on the Federal side. In the markets where things were still normal, they bought essential items that were no longer available in Biafra as a result of embargoes. Sometimes the traders would be gone for weeks and nobody knew if they were alive or dead. One day Money returned to find that her hometown had been sacked and her parents, three brothers, and four sisters had disappeared as if into thin air.

With nothing but her large basin of salt, onions, and small quantities of various necessities absent in the Biafra marketplace, she started the search for her family. With their disappearance, she lost the desire to risk her life for a few Biafran pounds. By the time her search brought her to Akasi, she had nothing left except the basin and a large bundle of Biafran money. She rented a room with a family in Oboro village. During her second week, she went to the relief office to ask for some salt. Mr. Eze was sorting stockfish in readiness for distribution that evening and asked her to help. A former secondary school teacher, he was a short, stocky man with a loud voice. Those who knew him before the war said he was a good chemistry teacher.

That first day he made it clear, without words, that neither Money's height nor her charming face would stop him from letting her go hungry if she didn't do the work he asked her to do. Over the past months, Money learned that Mr. Eze knew how to use his age privileges over the young and his education over the illiterate. That day, after she finished sorting the stockfish, he left with Father McManus for the village square. On her way back to Oboroji, she saw the relief workers at the village square and went to help with the distribution.

That was how she began work at the relief office. It was run jointly by the churches and the army base. When she wasn't working at the relief office, she helped at the checkpoint at the junction on the hill. Soon she was known in the nineteen villages as "that Army Girl."

Money finished sorting the stockfish. She found some twine and tied the open end of each grayish-brown sack. The smell of stockfish was strong in the storeroom, which doubled as Mr. Eze's office. Piles of sacks bulging with food and assorted donated items from foreign countries reached the ceiling on one side of the room. On weekends Mr. Eze opened some of the sacks. Except for the food sacks, the contents were always a surprise. Sometimes the clothes were so tattered Mr. Eze could not bring himself to distribute them. Sometimes they were filled with heavy cold-weather clothes like winter coats, sweaters, and hats, which they could not distribute in the hot climate. Always, they smelled of a mixture of cornmeal, stockfish, and old sweat. Money kept hoping that one of these days they would find a pair of sandals that would fit her long, narrow feet. A handbag, too, would be helpful. A week before, Mr. Eze let her pick out a few dresses. Two of them were too nice for everyday wear. The others were too big for her slender frame. But she washed all the dresses carefully and placed them in a carton under her bed.

When she finished tying the sacks, she called some of the

boys who were always around the mission, waiting for some work and a small gift or two that would help alleviate the hunger in their bellies and the starvation at home.

"Joe! David! Egwuatu! Come and put these in the car." The boys stopped their orange-ball soccer and came running. Before they went into Mr. Eze's office, they wiped the sticky rotten-orange juices from their legs and feet with leaves from the hedge of blooming lantana and began to load the bulging food sacks into the boot and back seat of the Ford. When they finished, she gave each of them some cornmeal, a cigarette-cupful of rice, and a piece of stockfish.

"Thank-you-Miss," they said one after the other as they clutched the precious packets.

"Now, go home. I'm sure your parents need help with work at the farm."

"Yes, Miss." The boys sauntered off. Watching them leave, she pushed the thought of her brothers to the furthest recesses of her mind.

She threw three old cigarette cups and a notebook into a small enamel bucket. The cups were for measuring the cornmeal and the occasional rice rations. Outside she placed the bucket on the ground near the little Ford and waited. Soon, Father McManus and Mr. Eze came out of the rectory. Father's white soutane billowed a little in the warm breeze. His freckled face was red from long hours under the African sun; as usual, his brown hair was ruffled.

"Why you no enter car?" Father asked as he looked with mock dismay at the car, which was sagging from the weight of the sacks. Money smiled noncommittally, showing pearly white teeth. She squeezed into the back seat, the bucket on her lap. Soon they were at the village square.

Although the place was teeming with people, the crowd was subdued. People spoke in low voices, even whispers, as they waited for the relief rations. Money knew that some of these people had not tasted salt in their food for weeks. Father drove slowly, gently parting the crowd as the Ford inched its way to the far end of the square, where a large table was set up. The rest of the relief volunteers were already standing behind the table. The shame of begging for food kept the crowd restrained. People refused to meet each other's eyes. Some parents, not wanting to witness the humiliated gazes of friends and relatives, sent their children. Those children who were too sick to be sent or left at home stood in line, their emaciated forms hanging like death on the waists of mothers or older sisters. Like the ghosts of the children their mothers had hoped would one day join in the games on the village playground, the sick children were a burdensome presence in this crowd, which was waiting for relief from a war whose cause they did not yet understand. Many of the children were two, five, six, nine years old, and hunger was eating them alive in the presence of their parents. Their shiny, distended middles and thin, frail limbs spoke the fear in the faces of the healthy children in the crowd. A small number of the sick were adults forced to fend for themselves in a community where everyone usually cared for the needy and elderly. Before the war, nobody had ever heard of *kwashiorkor*. Now it was almost a household word. Women asked each other about it.

"How are you?"

"We are still breathing. My trading has stood still since the road to Atani market closed."

"How are the children?"

"They are alive. Only the little one, Ugo, has been sick lately."

"Is it regular sickness or the war disease?"

"I don't know, my sister. She has not been eating well."

"You should take her to the relief people. Their cornmeal cures everything. Mix it with that powdered milk they give you and she will be able to eat and play again in no time."

"I will go and see, my sister. May the day break!"

The conversations buzzed in subdued tones around the relief table. Money and the other workers deftly measured cigarette-cupfuls of cornmeal, rice, or powdered milk into bowls, cups, carefully folded plantain leaves, and even outstretched hands. Sometimes, they gave the occasional Excedrin or Bufferin for general body aches. Two of the workers, trying to keep count of how many people were receiving aid, placed tally marks on notebook paper.

Father went around, talking to people, telling them to come to church. But today, his ever-ready smile looked forced in this crowd. It was not only this village square. There were other relief tables all over Akasi. What did one feed thousands of sick, hungry people resigned to fear and capricious killings? Last week, when the number of people in the relief line reached an all-time low, he met with the village heads and asked them to make announcements about kwashiorkor. Those not killed by the bullets must not be allowed to die in their homes. He told the village heads to ask the people to come out and get food from the relief people at the village square. The chiefs had told him that hunger was not the problem. The war was. Could he and his God end it? Besides, it was more risky for everyone to be in one place at the same time because of air raids and the constantly changing war fronts. Also, how did they know that he, a white man, was not a saboteur? He tried talking to the Presbyterian and Methodist pastors. They were locals. But they too seemed to have given up hope. Today, Father McManus was working hard, trying to reach the people he knew were behind these war masks, the people he had come to serve in this warm-hearted African town.

"Father! Father!"

"Father, Money is calling you. Father."

The girl, Money, was waving for him to go back to the table.

"Father, food don' finish-o."

"Alright. Mek we go bring more chop. Tell people, no go!" He revved the Ford engine and left with two young men. Within a half hour, they returned with more bulging sacks of food. Mr. Eze was angry. He had been supervising relief distribution for months. Never had he seen this many people. Always he had made sure that the people he knew would get food. Sometimes he was harsh to the uneducated farm women whose husbands and children he did not know, forcing them to leave without food or salt.

"Our food is finished for today," he would say, rubbing his hands together and clapping them in an exaggerated manner to show how empty the sacks were. "Go home and take care of your husbands and children."

The women, doubly humiliated, would leave with averted eyes. It was rumored that Mr. Eze sold some of the food and used clothing to traders from nearby towns. Today his short legs could barely carry him as he ran back and forth, trying to control the already subdued crowd. In his nice clothes, he exuded a well-being that ill matched the palpable poverty and desperation of most of the people at the square.

"Move back from the table!" he shouted over and over. "How can our people be so shameless? Why won't they go to work?" Mr. Eze fumed at no one in particular.

"It is not the work," one of the women relief workers said. Her husband was a prominent businessman even in the Emergency. Mr. Eze stopped to look at her. No one could mistake the venom in the look he gave her. Secure in her knowledge of his inability to do anything other than glower at her, she continued, "Our women are hard workers. But when you have nothing to cook with, what is there to work for? What is the point of working all day when there is no salt in people's lives?"

"Mr. Eze, please come and help me open this sack." Money was struggling to open a stubborn sack of powdered milk.

"Who do you think I am? Your servant?" Mr. Eze strode over to the table, happy to find an outlet for his frustration. But Money was too intent on the annoying sack to hear Mr. Eze's mounting anger.

"Mr. Eze! I said, ple——"

"I said I am not your servant, you harlot!" The air around the table resounded with the slap. Money blinked back the tears. Although her fingers itched to touch her cheek, she knew that even moving her hands toward her face would unleash the sobs. The silence spread slowly through the crowd.

"Look!" one child said to his mother, "Teacher Eze slapped Money."

"Wait!" one of the women shouted, "Okoronkwo Eze slapped Army Girl!"

"What did she do?" Hushed voices soon became an angry hum.

"Why didn't he join the army, if he knows how to fight?"

"No. Don't you know he can only beat women?"

"Doesn't he know she's a refugee?" Someone quickly led Mr. Eze into a nearby compound. Slowly people dispersed. Some vowed to never go near the relief office again.

"If education brings only war and disrespect, may I never be seen anywhere near your book houses," one old woman was heard to say.

The next day Father McManus told Mr. Eze that he was no longer the head of the relief office. Money was to take care of relief until further notice. Mr. Eze was put in charge of first-aid training at the hospital.

Instead of just going in to sort stockfish and other items and help with distribution, Money also made the trips to wherever relief headquarters happened to be. Unlike Mr. Eze, she couldn't drive and had to have a driver assigned to her.

One of the soldiers from the base was assigned as her driver and guard. Because of the threat of air attacks, the army truck could take her to headquarters only early in the morning, before sunrise. They would load up the truck at intervals during the day and return to Akasi at night. In the hilly countryside, the journey was dangerous because the driver could not drive with full headlights on, for fear of night ambushes. Money's reputation as the army girl grew even though people received more food at the village squares. In a few months, she moved into two rooms. The carpenter made some chairs for her new place.

Money continued her inquiries about her family. She still worked at the checkpoint on the hill, and every time a new batch of refugees came through, she would be heard shouting the names of her brothers and sisters into the crowds of desolate strangers huddled in the trucks or milling down the road.

Every so often someone would say, "What are your parents' names? Mr. and Mrs. What?"

"They're not Mr. and Mrs. Anything," she would say. "They're not educated."

"Then how are you going to find them?"

"Their friends called them Nne Money or Nna Money. I was their first child," she said simply. "They are my parents. Some of my brothers and sisters look like me. We look like our father. They were farm people. But I don't know what they are doing now. They might even be dead."

"I will ask around," would be the answer. Although the voices of the people she asked held out some hope, there was always a certain vagueness in their promises to help that made it difficult for Money to hope. But she hoped.

One day at relief headquarters, one of the soldiers said in answer to her query about her family, "Aren't you Father McManus's girlfriend? You live in Akasi, don't you? I know Mr. Eze."

Money sat down right there at the relief office and cried. She did not know what to say. A woman in an Emergency Army uniform came up and held her.

"Don't cry, my sister. We are all someone's girlfriend, wife, or daughter. What is the problem?"

"I don't know. I just want to know where my people are. I haven't done anything to anybody." Money sobbed even harder. The woman continued to hold her until she calmed down.

Later, Money told her about her lost family. The woman's name was Mrs. Grace Okon. She was from Onitsha area and had married an Ibibio man. When the war broke out, her husband sent her home to his people while he stayed in Lagos to finish up some things about their business. On his way back he was killed in a car accident near Benin. When the news of his death came, his people almost killed her and her three children. They called her a wicked Uneñe woman. She escaped with the children at night. But they walked into an ambush near Aba. All the children were killed. She escaped and eventually joined the military police.

"I thought you're army," Money said softly.

"No. I have this uniform because they didn't have my size in the police ones when I needed a replacement."

"Thank you. Looking at you, no one would ever guess the load you're carrying," Money said.

"It's nothing. If your people are alive, you will find them one of these days. Give me everybody's names and I'll help you ask more people."

Money gave Mrs. Okon the names. Later she took Money to the back of headquarters, where she had a room. They had a lunch of rice and stewed stockfish. On the way home that evening, Money felt more relieved than she had in a long time. But life at Akasi continued uneventfully. In August, Father McManus left. His replacement, a younger man from Bristol, kept everything the way it was. Money continued working at the relief office. Her work hours grew longer as the war fronts grew closer. The number of dialects spoken by her clientele increased. Sometimes she would be at the office all day, doling out food, used clothing, basic painkillers, and a few kind words in between. Some days, because of the long line at the office, she couldn't make it to the village square and had to send the driver by himself. She continued to look for her family among the crowds of refugees. Sometimes someone would raise her hopes. One day someone told her that he had seen her parents and that he had heard they had died during an air attack on a refugee camp. She cried inconsolably until the same man came back and told her he heard that the attack had been on a different camp. But he couldn't tell her where her parents were. Money continued to hope.

In November she went to pick up some relief from headquarters. The drive up there was slow as usual. When they arrived, just before sunrise, the place was deserted. Money waited in the office, wondering what to do. Mrs. Okon ran in and told her and the driver to go with her into the forest. She said she had run all the way because she remembered that Money was supposed to come in that morning. Money and Jude, the driver, left with her. On the way into the nearby forest, Mrs. Okon told them that they were expecting an attack on the relief headquarters. One of the Affia-attack women had told them two days before that they had seen some enemy soldiers coming this way. They were heavily armed and on foot. They talked about destroying the civilians' main food source. So headquarters was ready. The place was surrounded by emergency soldiers waiting for the ambush. The soldiers let Mrs. Okon through, telling her to make sure she got Money and Jude out quickly.

Throughout that day they waited for the attack. The enemy soldiers did not come. By evening people began to trickle back into the base. At about nine o'clock the relief plane arrived. Money had never seen one this close before and went to see.

"Be careful," Mrs. Okon said. "The danger is not over yet. They can still attack."

"Thank you. Nothing will happen to me."

"You won't be able to see anything. They're unloading into the other building tonight because of the expected attack."

"I won't go far. I'm just going to stand out here. You will hear me if I scream."

Outside, the moon was out and Money could make out the soldiers' silhouettes as they went back and forth between the building and the plane. The small plane had landed in the middle of the soccer field. From where she stood in the shadow of the large relief headquarters, Money could see the men going back and forth. She wanted to go up to the pilot and ask to see the inside but could not find the courage to leave the shadow that sheltered her from the soldiers' view. Suddenly an arm was flung over her shoulder and a hand over her mouth.

"Hello, Miss." It was James Oha, the soldier who had asked her if she was Father McManus's girlfriend.

"Don't say anything," he whispered roughly. "Just come with me peacefully or I'll shoot you." He began to pull her toward the far end of the building, away from the quiet bustle near the airplane. She was about his height and could smell his breath. He had been drinking but he was not yet drunk. He kept talking, hinting at how much she was going to enjoy what he was going to show her. She waited until they were almost at the end of the building. As they turned the corner, his grip around her shoulder relaxed just a little.

She ducked out of the half-circle of his amorous embrace and bent all the way to her strapless sandals. She grabbed one sandal and slapped him across the eyes with it. Blinded for a moment, he reached for his gun. She hooked a knee into his groin, causing him to double over in pain. By the time he recovered, she was halfway toward the airplane. He fired. She felt something sting her left thigh. Still running, she slid her foot out of the other sandal. The pilot and his mate were in the cockpit and for that short minute the soldiers were all inside the building. Shoeless, she hoisted herself into the plane and stumbled into the cabin. Something warm and wet tickled her heels as she slid behind a large box.

"Is everything on the ground then?" the pilot asked. He thought it was one of the soldiers. Money said nothing. She crawled between the seats just as the first shot rang out.

"It's an attack!"

"Attack! Attack!" More voices joined in the alarm.

"Jesus! They're serious. Move it, Fred!" As more shots rang out into the cool night, the plane's engine came to life.

"Move, man! Let's get out of here! These Africans are going to blow us to tarnation." The plane moved a few feet and soared into the night.

About fifteen minutes later, Fred went into the cabin.

"Jesus, men. We have cargo!"

"What do you mean we have cargo?"

"Here she is."

"She? What the . . . Where you from, gal?"

Money looked at the two men. Her face was without expression. Something about her face stirred a memory in the one called Fred.

"What's you name, gal?" he asked gruffly. Who would have thought that working for Uncle Sam would get him into this many close brushes with death and accidental acts of kindness.

"Money. My name is Money." She braced herself for the bullet.

"No kidding. You're Money?" He exchanged surprised glances with his mate. They burst into laughter. The plane continued its drone into the night sky.

"Are you related to Chima?"

"Who is Chima?" Money asked without thinking.

"Chima. His brother's name is Solomon. They're like twins. They said they have a sister named Money and have been asking us to bring her out of the war. No matter. Maybe it's just a coincidence."

"Chima and Sol?" Money's face became animated.

"Yes, Sol. That's what the parents call him. Do you know them?"

Money fell on her knees. Then she doubled over and gave in to all the tears she had not shed in the past year. Fred brought her some water.

"Here, drink this. Do you know them?"

"Yes. They're my brothers."

"Good. We're going back to Gabon. Your family is all there. We airlifted them there a few months back. There had been an attack on a refugee camp . . ."

Money did not hear the rest. Her joy-filled tears complemented the drone of the small airplane as it sliced through the cool night air.

Osondu

The lull in the gunfire exchange had upgraded itself to a temporary cease-fire. Both sides decided to take a few days' break. Occasionally, someone fired a few shots to make sure that the other side was not planning any surprises.

Osondu sat in the trenches. His entire body itched. He took advantage of the break to kill as many lice as he could in the folds of his tattered uniform. The three stripes on his uniform barely hung onto his shoulders. It was useless. His clothes had just enough loose threads to harbor an army of lice. But Osondu was hopeful. The expected medical team would bring some soap and fresh clothes. At least they would bring some Dettol for the bites on his back, belly, and thighs. His stomach grumbled. He hadn't eaten a decent meal in a long time.

He was part of an emergency rescue operation in the Biafran army. For the past three weeks his troop had been covering this stretch of the Cross River because the regular troop was almost wiped out the month before. The men who had survived the ordeal still suffered nightmares, and every few days several of them were removed to the hospital in Akasi, about twenty miles away. Today a fresh batch of soldiers was expected, along with some medical supplies and uniforms. Soon, Osondu's troop would move to another front. The trenches here were unhealthy, more so than at any fronts he had seen before. Despite the dry season, these trenches, which were close to the riverbanks, were often muddy, slowly filling up with marshy water. When it rained, the men on guard duty had to take off their boots and stand knee-deep in the mud. No matter how often he went on these rescue operations, Osondu could not adjust to them. He loved the ambushes, the attacks. But he could never get used to the surprises posed by the landscape. During the rainy season the ground was soaking wet, vomiting slippery reddish-brown mud. In the dry season, just looking at the sun-cracked earth increased your thirst and made you long for the mud. On those days he broke off pieces of dry earth to eat in the hope that he would be able to squeeze some forgotten moisture from it. But today Osondu was tired of the filth and the unforgiving hunger that squeezed his stomach. He looked forward to the next deployment.

The medical truck arrived late in the afternoon and the soldiers lined up for supplies. They were tired and hungry and their uniforms barely hung on their emaciated frames. Osondu waited in the trenches as one then another of his friends went up to the truck for a few minutes before returning to their positions. When it was his turn Osondu went to the truck. His leisurely gait belied his excitement about fresh supplies. The healthy-looking officer standing at the makeshift table of the truck's tailgate was impeccably dressed; the creases on his uniform were razor sharp. Simultaneously the two men's faces broke into wide grins as they recognized each other. Osondu couldn't believe his eyes. The emergency medical officer was a classmate from his secondary school days.

"Good afternoon. Mike, you no remember me?"

"Osondu! This na ya' eye?" Mike held out his hand.

Osondu gripped Mike's hand in a tight handshake. His eyes swept Mike's features admiringly. Mike looked every inch the army officer. Osondu tried hard not to show his reaction to the clean, starched, well-ironed uniform with shining buttons. The shiny brown boots.

"Na me be dis, my broda," Osondu laughed.

Mike examined Osondu quickly. He gave him a new first aid pack and swabbed his rashes and bites with disinfectant. To Osondu the Dettol smelled like expensive perfume. He inhaled deeply. When Mike finished, Osondu put on his shirt.

"Thank you, my brother."

"Sorry, we don't have much of anything left. Your people are doing a good job guarding the front lines." He held out his hand for a farewell. As the men's hands gripped again, an explosion followed a quick flash of light, and flying shrapnel enveloped the world. Caught by surprise, the two men could not even duck as their hold on each other's hands tightened. When Osondu opened his eyes, Mike's head was gone, and not one man from the medical team was in sight. Osondu extricated himself from the handshake and dove into the bushes as Mike's headless body fell with a dull thud to the ground.

Osondu ran to his position in the trench, firing blindly. After about an hour the captain called for a retreat.

"Pull out! Pull out! Now!"

Osondu stumbled out of the trench. Was that fear he heard in the captain's voice? Osondu started to retreat in line with his comrades. The automatic rifle in his hands seemed to have a life of its own.

But the well-armed troops on the other side of the river were advancing steadily, and Osondu's unit was unable to hold out. The enemy troops sounded like they had just received supplies enough for two armies. Osondu soon ran out of bullets and started to run. Chidi, who usually was next to him in line, began to cover him.

"They're still coming!"

"Run, Osondu, run!"

Osondu headed for cover in the nearby forest. All around him men were running; some lay on the ground, moaning in pain. He thought he heard one of the fallen men call his name and he stopped.

"Run, Osondu! Hold down your head. Run!" someone shouted as a bullet flashed by his ear.

"My mother, they have killed us." Chidi's voice rang out over the din as he continued to cover Osondu's retreat. Finally he, too, ran.

"Move! Move! Don't give up! Fire!" the captain's voice continued to cajole in the midst of the men's retreat. Another explosion caught a group of men, including the captain, sending more shrapnel and body parts flying. Dust and smoke billowed. More men fell. Others ran. It was everyone for himself.

Osondu and Chidi ran until the exchange of gunfire was far behind them. Although occasionally an explosion caused them to stop briefly to get their bearings, the two men ran until they were exhausted. Soon the forest around them yielded no more human voices, no more commands to fire or retreat. No screams of anguish, pain, or terror. Osondu and Chidi sat down at the foot of a big tree. Pieces of blue sky peeked through the leaves in the forest's roof. Far away a passenger plane droned.

"Do you know where we are?" Chidi asked. He was a sergeant in the Emergency Army also.

"No. I've never been this far down this river."

"I think we are near one of those Akasi farm plantations."

"You think Akasi people own land this far away from home?"

"Yes. This one belongs to Umuiwe. The farmers move here during the planting and harvesting seasons because it's too far to travel back and forth daily."

"I've never seen a farm plantation before. How far away is it?"

"Two or three miles. My mother is from Umuiwe. When I was younger I used to come here with my cousins. We set traps for animals and picked mushrooms in this forest." Chidi stood up. "Let's go."

Chidi led the way. Osondu followed. Brought up in the city, he did not understand how Chidi could be so sure of where they were. Although he could feel the depth of the forest, each tree looked equally big. He thought he heard a rustle behind him and turned. But no one was there. He hurried until he was only a step behind Chidi, almost stepping on his heels. Without his gun, Osondu was afraid. The image of Mike's well-dressed, headless body kept coming back.

"We're almost there," Chidi said reassuringly.

"What's that smell?"

"It's probably an animal caught in a trap a few days ago." Chidi dismissed the question with a wave of his hand. "We're here."

They stepped out of the forest as suddenly as if a door had been opened ahead of them. Osondu caught his breath.

"It's a whole town!"

"I told you, it's an Umuiwe farm plantation."

"I didn't know it would be a whole village with corrugated-iron-roofed houses."

"Some of the farmers spend more than half the year here. It's an extension of their village. Go that way. I'll look over on the other side of the compound."

Osondu was unprepared for this village tucked in the middle of the forest. But more disturbing was the quiet. The stench grew stronger, heightening the silence. The absence of children's voices, of noises from goats, chickens, or sheep, ruffled the late afternoon heat. Osondu felt the goose bumps prickle his skin. He strained to regain his soldiering skills. The thatched roofs on the row houses on either side of the compound looked intact. But there were bullet holes in the beautifully decorated walls. The walls of the stand-alone corrugated-iron-roofed houses in the middle of the compound were also riddled with bullet holes. Resolutely he walked behind some of the houses in search of the source of the pervasive smell.

"My father, they have killed me!"

Osondu hurried toward Chidi's voice. There were bullet-riddled bodies in various positions of death in the middle of the compound. There were men and women and children. Many were no longer recognizable. Evidently it was a surprise attack. How else could one explain so many dead in one place in a civilian village?

"What are we going to do? Look at the flies, they're so big!"

"We have to bury whatever the flies haven't already consumed." Chidi crossed himself.

"The flies are so full, they're no longer buzzing. Look, they're just hanging with distended stomachs."

"Whoever did this must not be human. Come on, let's find some hoes."

They searched the houses looking for something to dig with.

"The killers must have looted the place."

"Maybe not," said Chidi. He went into one of the row houses. "If they were soldiers, they probably left soon after. Perhaps people from one of the nearby towns did the looting. Even the hoes and machetes are gone." He reached up into the rafters in the front room.

"What are you doing?" Osondu stood at the door.

"I'm looking for a hoe. This is a woman's hut. Sometimes they put new hoes in the rafters. Look." He held up a shiny new hoe.

They found a second hoe in another hut and a machete in another. Working quickly, they fashioned crude handles for the hoes and began to dig large graves. They dug the graves in rows in front of the houses, just beyond the eaves. Six days later, they were still working. Chidi, always resourceful, looked for food in all the hiding places he could think of. The yam barns had been looted. In some of the houses they found some yams and cocoyams, which they boiled and ate with only salt and pepper. With not a bullet between them, they dared not go into the surrounding farmlands for fear of returning looters.

Every now and then Osondu thought he heard a rustle in the bushes behind the row houses. Each time, they went to look but found nothing. Both men were afraid but neither would admit his fear first. Without their commanding officers they were lost. So they took refuge in burying the dead. At night they slept in the bedroom of the biggest corrugated-iron-roofed house.

On the sixth afternoon they had just finished covering the last grave with red earth when they heard voices and heavy boots.

"Quick!" Chidi whispered. "Those are soldiers' footsteps."

They ran into one of the women's houses. As the voices came nearer, Osondu motioned for Chidi to climb into the rafters in the dark backroom. They had barely settled down in their hiding place when the new arrivals fired shots into the empty afternoon.

"Come out! Come out, now!" Boots stomped around the compound. More shots followed.

"The soil looks fresh. Maybe the diggers are still around," one of the soldiers said.

"Let's rest here for a while. Maybe they'll come back." The soldiers stopped for a while in front of the woman's hut where Osondu and Chidi were hiding. They spoke English with an accent from the far-off northern hills. Osondu and Chidi crouched lower in the rafters, hoping that their frame would not give way and reveal them. The enemy soldiers walked away, still talking loudly.

"Let's look around a little. The diggers may still be around."

"What if they're soldiers?" The two soldiers continued further into the compound. Two or three more voices joined them. Osondu and Chidi did not dare move a muscle. They heard the men decide to sit down at the other end of the compound to eat. Their laugher and conversation went far into the afternoon. Every so often they talked about waiting for the people who had dug the graves.

"Maybe they got tired and left."

"Maybe they're still around." Once or twice, a few of the men looked inside some of the houses. But with so many of the dead bodies still unburied and all the doors open, they could not convince themselves to make thorough searches. Toward evening they left in search of a more hospitable village. Osondu and Chidi stayed in their hiding place till dusk.

They continued digging for two more days. Osondu talked frequently about that last handshake with Mike's well-dressed, headless body.

"I'll never forget that day. Imagine me. Shaking hands with the dead," he said one afternoon, swiping at a large fly. The men had sat down for a few minutes to rest. The flies, deprived of their meals of rotting flesh, were buzzing again.

"Many men would be glad to be in your shoes." Chidi wiped the sweat from his forehead with a grimy hand. Secretly he hoped they would finish burying all the bodies soon and start for home. Osondu must go through a ritual cleansing in the village if he is to come through this, he thought. But home was at least a day's walk away. With this war, who knew what lay between there and here?

"You have been privileged to see the connection between here and there. When we reach home you will be given a hero's welcome," Chidi said aloud.

"What kind of hero is that?" Osondu mocked. "You know, my great, great, great-grandfather was told the same thing when he came back from the great river."

"Hmm?" Chidi was not sure what to say. Stories about the past and the great river filled him with dread. He reached for his roughly made hoe, ready to get back to the work at hand. Osondu didn't move.

"You know, one of my ancestors was kidnapped by the Aro traders. They took him to the mouth of the great river. There he saw many others who were being taken to the *oshimiri ukwu*, the big water. When they untied them so they could empty their bowels and bladders, he managed to hide away in the night. Luckily he had traveled to the market near the great river a few times before and could find his way home. That was when my family moved to Akasi. Our name was changed to Osondu."

"I always thought that that was a strange name for these parts."

"All the people came out to welcome him. He was gone for a whole planting season. They gave him a ritual bath on his father's grave, cleansing him of all the bad things that may have touched him while he was gone. They renamed him so the kidnappers would be unable to find him again." Osondu's story seemed to have transported him to a remembered past that Chidi knew nothing about.

"The ritual bath must have worked."

"Yes, it did. But it must have worked only for him. Every generation since has found my people looking for one child or the other, or waiting for some family member to return."

"Except for you. You are here."

They went back to work. The hole was getting deeper and the soil was softer, making their work a little easier in the blazing January sun.

"I heard that rustle again." Osondu stood up quickly.

"Don't move then." Chidi did not even look up. "Keep working. Try not to look in the direction of the noise," he said under his breath.

"What are you talking about? I said I heard that noise again."

"Climb out slowly. We'll see who it is today."

Osondu climbed out of the hole and sat down on the warm, loose soil they had heaped on the ground nearby. They hoped this would be the last grave. Chidi continued to dig, carefully piling loose soil near Osondu's feet.

"Nna-a? Wetin now? Come, mek we go look now." Osondu was getting impatient.

Chidi continued to dig. Then they heard it—a series of those low notes that women use to call each other in the farmlands. Before they could move, Osondu was knocked back into the unfinished grave. He landed on Chidi.

"Quick! Hurry! Cover them!"

Chidi heard them from far away. "Quick! Elebuo! Ejituru! Hurry."

"No. Stop! Elebuo! It's me." Clumps of soil fell on Chidi's head and back. He struggled to a sitting position spitting out soil as he raised his hands in surrender. More soil fell on his head.

"Biko! Ejituru! It's me. Chidi, the son of Nne Okezie!" He spat again, not daring to lower his hands.

"They're saying something. Stop," one of the women said.

"No. Don't stop. They will kill us."

"They will kill us today. Look at all the people they have killed and buried."

Chidi wiped the soil from his face. Osondu, still face down, was almost completely covered with red soil. "Wait. Elebuo. Wait!"

"Elebuo. They know you. Wait!"

Elebuo looked. Finally, she recognized Chidi's face under the dust and grime.

"Chineke will not agree with a bad thing. It's my brother. Chidi." The women stopped shoving red soil into the grave.

"Chidi, is that you?"

"Yes. But you have buried Osondu alive."

"Who? Where is he?"

"Mama Osondu's son. Wait." Chidi was scooping red soil aside. He pulled Osondu up by the hand. Osondu spat out some soil and fell back. The women helped pull him out of the hole. They started to dust the soil from his face and hair. Soon he was breathing smoothly again.

"What happened? Where did you come from?" the men asked.

"One of the women saw you the day before the war ended," said Elebuo.

"The war ended?" The two men looked at each other in disbelief.

"Yes. Didn't you know?"

"Back home, they think you're dead or that you went AWOL."

"Yes, they say that most of the people in your group died."

"You didn't know the war is finished?"

"Would we be here if we knew that?" Chidi asked.

"One of the women saw you the day before the war ended. She didn't know who you were. She came home and told us that the soldiers who killed all our people were back. People have been watching you ever since. We were waiting for the rest of your friends to come so we could get all of you. One day they came but left before we could do anything."

"Those were not our men. They were enemy soldiers."

"But you said that the war is over?" Chidi said the words slowly, carefully. As if he did not want to understand what they meant.

"Yes. But only in the towns and villages. Enemy soldiers are still going around killing people."

"But how did you get here? There must be at least one war front between here and home."

"There are two. But this is our land. Our cassava, cocoyams, and yams are here."

"Do your husbands know that you've been coming here?" Osondu could not believe what he was hearing.

"They know we go to the farm. Yes." The women were matter-of-fact in their acceptance of their wartime responsibilities.

"This is our land. The soldiers are only doing their job. We have children to feed."

"And the war is over?"

"Yes. It was easy to watch you."

"Do you know who killed them?" one of the women asked, waving her hands over the red earth mounds.

"Some soldiers coming through the bush. These people they killed are those who came here to hide from the air raids on the villages. They're mostly women with babies and older men and women. Some of them arrived here one morning, a week or so before the war ended. Many people thought that these plantations are safer because they're far away from the hustle and bustle of village life. Now they are all dead. We have been watching. Waiting to see if there were more enemy soldiers. Two market weeks before Okom saw you, Ejituru and myself saw about six soldiers wearing the uniforms of the Federal troops. We hid in the cassava farms on the other side of the stream to wait. They usually will pass. But these ones did not. After a while we heard the shootings. We didn't worry too much. Sometimes they shot our goats and chickens for their people at the front. But that day, when we came back, they were gone and all the people were dead. What are you going to do?" Ejituru looked at the men with shining steel eyes. She had no more tears to shed.

"First, let's finish this last one. Then we'll find something to eat," Chidi replied.

"Tomorrow, we'll go home," Osondu added.

They worked quickly. With the women's help, the work went faster. After they covered the last hole completely, the women found some *abosi* leaves for ritual cleansing. Standing in turn on the most recent mound of red earth, the young men took off their dirty, tattered shirts for the ritual bath of the healing words of their townswomen.

When it was over, Elebuo said, "We're glad to have you back with us, in the land of the living. The elders will do the rest. You'll be given a welcome fit for heroes."

Later the women went back into the forest for some yams they had hidden from the soldiers. They found pepper, salt, and oil in places Chidi and Osondu thought they had looked before. The women laughed at their surprise, joking about men who didn't know where to look for things that make life worth living. By the time they finished cooking, the sun had gone down. They all sat in the front room of one of the corrugated-iron-roofed houses as the two young men ate their first good meal in months.

The Gift

My life is a small prayer answered beyond my mother's expectations. She had prayed hard for a child.

"Any child," she sighed. She poured libation at every opportunity. Soon, with my grandfather's firm guidance, every family member at home and abroad poured libation.

"Give Mgbore-nta a child for us. Any child," they intoned between crunchy kola nuts and cupfuls of sweet palm wine.

Yet she was not sure if prayers by people like her were ever answered. Her tall, comely frame began to droop in anticipation of unfulfilled womanhood. Imagine her joy when I came along.

Onyinye she called me—"Gift." Over the years she called forth the gift in me. I responded, not knowing what she wanted from me.

"I do not have a gift," I protested.

"No, my child. You do not have a gift. You are a gift given to everyone you meet. You will bear untold gifts to those who ask. Do not worry yourself about having a gift! Obioma. That is the road." She took the handkerchief I was sewing for needlework class from me and smoothed the rough edges of the green leaves with yellow flowers. Her ebony-smooth skin shone in the late afternoon light. "Our people say that those who have a good heart become the door through which a community sees its dreams come true. I am a poor woman and can give you nothing except the words of the ancestors."

Still, I did not understand. I struggled to find the gift that I thought my mother saw in me. Some days I went to the market to see her on my way back from school. Between mouthfuls of hot, peppery *akara* or salt-sweetened groundnuts, I would ask her again about my names.

"Does Nneka mean I'll be great?" I would look deep into her eyes, trying to see into her future and mine.

"Do not worry about being great. Greatness comes from you and your *chi*. I wanted to be a mother. When you came to us, that made me great. Our people say that Mother is supreme." She showed me how to wrap the pepper and dried fish in old newspapers and give correct change, how to haggle with customers and smile.

"It is only market, not a fight. The market woman who is never asked what she has to sell is a poor trader indeed."

"But I am not a mother."

"No, you are not. But Nneka is your other name."

"I don't want to be a mother." I was thirteen and willful.

"I know," my mother said. "You don't have to be a mother to know Nneka. Nne refers to all that you come from. It is all your kinship, the land, our people."

It took me many years to feel Akasi, our hometown, as Nne. I knew that Akasi was Nne one day on my way home from Aba, where we lived. As the hills and valleys sped by, I felt Ebube, wonder-spirit of the land. I wanted to shout my joy that I belonged to them. That day I wanted to fly over the hills and valleys. But I could only fly alongside the taxi that was speeding us toward Akasi, the Mother.

We spent Christmas, the harvest season, in Akasi. We attended noisy weddings and visited Nenne, my grandmother. I told her about Nneka and my flight over the hills and valleys. She ululated and danced her spirit dance.

"I always knew you would one day understand it," Nenne said. But I still did not understand it. I only knew it. I asked my cousin Nneka about it. She was fifteen.

"Don't listen to them," she said, sniffing. "They call me Nne only when I have done something wrong. When Father calls me Nne in that voice, I feel that I have to run away from him. I wish I could fly like you did."

On our way back to Aba, just after we passed Umuahia, I remembered my friends Ohabueze and Uloma, brother and sister who lived next door to us. Again I felt the Nneka flight in me. Aba was also home. After that day, I looked forward to the flights home to all Igboland. I waited for flights to Onitsha, Enugu, Asaba, Orlu, Ugwuta. In my dreams I flew to the Nneka places of my birth. Sometimes the knowledge of flight came at me from the voices of classmates, age-mates who were also in the process of self-recognition. Imagine my surprise when we went to Lagos for the first time to visit my uncle and I felt the Nneka-surge at Ikeja motor park. I laughed out loud.

"What is it?" my mother asked.

"Nneka. Nneka is Nigeria," I squealed my surprise.

The people sitting near us in the bus said, "*Ekene dili chukwu.* The young shall grow."

They said, "Our children understand the land. Long live Nigeria!"

"*Iheoma agwu-agwu,*" said my mother, embracing me. "Nigeria is good. She will live long if you keep knowing Nneka."

I began to feel the closeness between my mother and me in a new way. Some days it felt like the closeness between her and Nenne. The closeness between her and Nenne is endless. Especially when they quarrel. Then my father, brothers, and I say to each other, "Mama and Nenne are quarreling."

"It's the quarrel between kinsfolk. It doesn't reach the bone," my father would say.

Later, I found out he was wrong. When Nigeria quarreled with her children, people died. Unlike the quarrels between Nenne and Mama, the one between Nigeria and her children shook the earth and rent the sky in pieces. I could not go to

Ikeja motor park again without fear. I prayed for safety in Ekeoha market, Dugbe, Otu-Onicha, Ogba-ete. I could no longer fly over the hills and valleys. The rivers stank from the floating dead bodies of my kinsfolk. There was nothing to drink. I could no longer fly because strange birds flew our skies, sending lightning streaks that stopped the Nneka dream-flights of Nigerian daughters in mid-air.

"*Iheoma n'agwu-agwu*—good things do end." I told my mother she had lied to me. Where was the Nneka-dream of our people? There could be no more future in Nigeria, the Mother. Sadness, misery, and death walked the land.

"You say I am telling stories? Yes, I am a storyteller. Those were nightmare flights into the endless depths of darkness. The days dawned the same as they had for our ancestors. The sun shone for us the same as it had for them. But our fathers had not learned from their fathers how our ancestors accepted a pact of kinship between Igbos, Hausas, Yorubas, Efiks, Tivs, Ogonis . . . They blamed our ancestors for agreeing to kinship across hills and valleys, forests and grasslands, streams and rivers, instead of decimation by colonization."

"Why did they do it? We are not related to these people. What kind of nonsense is that?"

"No'sinse?" asked Nenne. Angered, she spoke the English words she had paid for my father to learn. "No'sinse? What do you call no'sinse? *Ogo bu ikwu-ato*—in-laws are third kin. How do you deny your kin? We intermarried with other people from other parts before your One Nigeria."

"But One Nigeria is killing us."

"It will pass. *Nneji*—Mother holds together."

"I thought that means 'mother of yams.'"

"Yes when you say it like this, *Nne ji*. But it means the same thing. The mother of yams is the land." Nenne adjusted her lappa, ready to tell the story. "You see there was Eri . . ."

"Yes." I knew the story. "And he was at the beginning of

things. . . . We got the yam from the son and the cocoyam from the daughter."

"That is so." Nenne was patient. "But both came from the land. We are the soil and the soil is us. *Nneji oha*—Mother holds community together. Our land will grow us again and give us what we need to make her live long."

"But what if she forgets to . . ." I was doubtful. For days my mother's pot was tasteless. Our life was without salt. Our days were without dreams. I longed for the Nneka-dream days of my youth in a country where no man is oppressed. Where we stood in brotherhood in the midst of different tongues. A country that promised that Babel could never be a threat to its dreams should be able to provide for its children.

"*Ya gazie*—may it go well," my mother said. "I had a dream last night."

"What was it?" I was eager to hear about dreams in the nightmarish living of Nigeria's death quarrels with her children. Any dream was welcome.

"I dreamt there was an air raid."

"Oh." I was disappointed. I looked up into the bullet-streaking skies of our present-day Nigeria.

"No. Wait!" My mother was excited. "It's not what you think. I dreamt about an air raid. But instead of bombs and bullets, there were umbrellas. Many umbrellas. As they fell out of the airplane, the umbrellas unfolded and floated down to us. And they sheltered us from the plane! The pilots could not see us. I held one over you."

"You held an umbrella over me? But I am not a child any more."

"It is so," Nenne and my mother said together.

"You are Ezenwanyi—queenly woman," said my mother. "No, you are not a child anymore. You are queen of the rising sun. You will hold umbrellas over yourself and your children.

You. Onyinye. I see you rising. You will rise with the ancestors as they rose with the sun."

The following week peace returned. Nigeria rose and stretched. She stretched from Calabar to Lagos, from Benin to Sokoto to Kafanchan. Over the River Niger and the Benue, Nigeria stretched. Again.

My name is Onyinye. I have poured a libation to the ancestors. It may not be as powerful as my mother's, but it will add its power to hers. It will be part of the giving fruit of my mother's libation for my coming into being in her life of want in our land of peace and plenty.

Glossary

abosi	A kind of tree used to mark land boundaries in residential areas. Its leaves are used for several kinds of rituals.
achi	A large, shady tree.
aduduo	A tree that blooms in the dry season (variant: *oha*).
agodo	A mud bed whose hollow middle is covered with slabs of lightweight wood.
agwu	A deity known for its powers of spirit-possession.
akara	Deep-fried cakes made from black-eyed peas.
balli	A kind of shoe for girls.
biko	Please.
camwood	A soft, red, perfumed wood used to make a red body lotion.
chi	Personal god.
Chineke	God; God-the-creator.
cigarette cup	Cigarettes used to come in aluminum tins, which are still used as a "cup" measure in many West African markets.
cocoyam	A tropical plant with broad leaves and a starchy, edible tuber.
dibia	Medicine man, indigenous doctor.
egusi	A type of melon grown in West Africa for its seeds.
Ekene dili chukwu	May God be thanked (lit., Thanks/gratitude belongs to God).

Ekpe	A secret society for men in southeastern Nigeria.
ekpo	Masquerade (southeastern Nigeria).
ezize	Brown powder from the perfumed roots of a shrub of the same name. Sometimes used instead of camwood.
fufu	Also *foo-foo*. A starch staple made from pounded west African yam, cocoyam, or cassava.
garri	Cassava flour.
george lappa	A *lappa* made in a plaid design. See *lappa*, below.
groundnut	A peanut.
Iheoma agwu-agwu	Good things never end.
jelof	West African rice dish made with fish or meat and tomatoes.
jigida	Girls' waist beads.
Kamalu	The god of thunder.
kwashiorkor	A form of malnutrition caused by a protein-deficient diet, especially in children.
lappa	A length of cloth worn around the waist by men and women.
maiden mask	Mask with the "face" and make-up of a young girl.
mammy wagon	A truck usually used to transport market women and their wares.
ndi-ichie	Ancestors.
nki	Scarification marks.
Nna	Father.
Nnaa-wo!	Good morning!
Nne	Mother.
nzuzu	A period of training and rest for girls who are about to get married.
oga	A children's clapping game.
ogbanje	Spirit-child(ren). Also the spirit that is said to possess such children.
ogbu n'igwe	Lit., "killer of masses (of people)."
ogwumabiri	The evening market.
okonko	A masquerade of the Ekpe secret society.

okro	Variant of *okra*.
stockfish	Dried codfish.
tanjele	Locally made mascara.
ugba	Oil bean seeds (also the tree).
ugu	West African pumpkin leaves.
Ugwu Awusa	Northern Nigeria (lit., the Hausa hills).
uke-mmuo	A spirit-child—see also *ogbanje*.
ukwu-achi	In the shade of the achi tree.
umunna	One's paternal kin.
Uneñe	Igbo (from Efik and Ibibio of southeastern Nigeria).
utasi	Tart-tasting leaf used for seasoning.
Vono bed	Trade name. Refers to any kind of bed with springs in the bed frame.
water-gift	Water that children fetch for relations and friends. Mandatory for *nzuzu* girls.
wrapper	See *lappa*. Used with standard English.